"We'll have separate bedrooms, of course..." Quent said, answering Amy's unspoken question

Then mischief glinted in his smile. "But we don't have to keep it that way. You might find having me around more tempting than you expect."

Amy didn't doubt that. She was all too aware of his muscular strength as he guided his car. But she reminded him, "We're doing this for the kids."

"You know I love them," he said.

Amy nearly stopped breathing until she heard the word *them*. For a moment she'd thought he was going to say he loved *her*. "I never saw you as the daddy type," she said unsteadily.

"People change," he answered.

"Yes, they do..." she murmured, wondering if he'd ever change enough to want to be a husband, as well as a father.

When that happened, she could only hope *she* was the one he fell in love with....

Dear Reader,

Our yearlong twentieth-anniversary celebration continues with a spectacular lineup, starting with *Saved by a Texas-Sized Wedding*, beloved author Judy Christenberry's 50th book. Don't miss this delightful addition to the popular series TOTS FOR TEXANS. It's a marriage-of-convenience story that will warm your heart!

Priceless Marriage by Bonnie Gardner is the latest installment in the MILLIONAIRE, MONTANA continuity series, in which a "Main Street Millionaire" claims her "ex" as her own. Jacqueline Diamond pens another charming story in THE BABIES OF DOCTORS CIRCLE series with *Prescription: Marry Her Immediately*. Here a confirmed bachelor doctor enlists the help of his gorgeous best friend in order to win custody of his orphaned niece and nephew. And let us welcome a new author to the Harlequin American Romance family. Kaitlyn Rice makes her sparkling debut with *Ten Acres and Twins*.

It's an exciting year for Harlequin American Romance, and we invite you to join the celebration this month and far into the future!

Melissa Jeglinski
Associate Senior Editor
Harlequin American Romance

PRESCRIPTION: MARRY HER IMMEDIATELY
Jacqueline Diamond

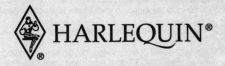

TORONTO • NEW YORK • LONDON
AMSTERDAM • PARIS • SYDNEY • HAMBURG
STOCKHOLM • ATHENS • TOKYO • MILAN • MADRID
PRAGUE • WARSAW • BUDAPEST • AUCKLAND

The author wishes to thank Marcia Holman for her
encouragement and her expert advice.

ISBN 0-373-16971-X

PRESCRIPTION: MARRY HER IMMEDIATELY

Visit us at www.eHarlequin.com

Printed in U.S.A.

ABOUT THE AUTHOR

The daughter of a doctor and an artist, Jacqueline Diamond claims to have researched the field of obstetrics primarily by developing a large range of complications during her pregnancies. She's also lucky enough to have a friend and neighbor who's an obstetrical nurse. The author of more than sixty novels, Jackie lives in Southern California with her husband and two sons. She loves to hear from readers. You can write to her at P.O. Box 1315, Brea, CA 92822, or by e-mail at JDiamondfriends@aol.com.

Books by Jacqueline Diamond

HARLEQUIN AMERICAN ROMANCE

HARLEQUIN INTRIGUE

*The Babies of Doctors Circle

Don't miss any of our special offers. Write to us at the following address for information on our newest releases.

Harlequin Reader Service
U.S.: 3010 Walden Ave., P.O. Box 1325, Buffalo, NY 14269
Canadian: P.O. Box 609, Fort Erie, Ont. L2A 5X3

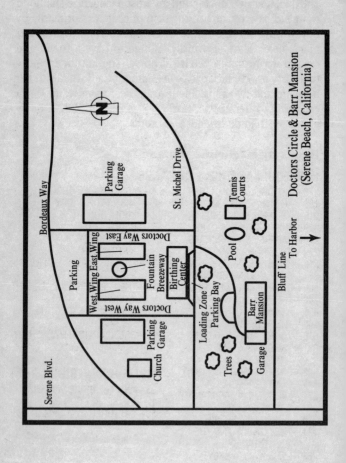

Doctors Circle & Barr Mansion
(Serene Beach, California)

Chapter One

The newborn waved her tiny fists as she lay along Dr. Quentin Ladd's arm with her head cradled in his hand. Her face, still red from the journey into life, quirked with a hint of a smile.

"Seven pounds, three ounces. Ten fingers and toes," he told her, and double-checked the name on the bassinet. "Lisa, you passed your first test with flying colors. Next stop, Harvard."

Baby-blue eyes blinked at him, not quite focusing. Then she sneezed.

"That's good," Quent said. "You can clear your airways with the best of them. I knew you were a winner."

He'd made a thorough test of her reflexes, heartbeat, breathing and other parameters. All normal. He was glad for her sake and for that of her numerous doting relatives, who had overflowed the waiting room during her birth.

It was one more happy event for Doctors Circle, a private hospital and clinic established in Serene Beach, California, to ensure the best care for mothers, would-be mothers and their babies. As a newly minted neo-natologist, Quent had been thrilled when he was invited to join the staff a couple of months ago.

While he was gently replacing the baby beneath her warmer light, Lisa's gaze connected, ever so briefly, with his. A sense of wonder spread through Quent as the little girl's future shimmered before him, from her first step to the day she would hold a baby of her own.

Where had all that come from? It wasn't as if he were going to be spending a lot of time with this particular infant, cute as she was. But it gave Quent a gut-level appreciation for the joy he saw on the faces of new fathers. Babies had always interested him from a clinical point of view, but lately he'd begun to take a more personal interest. This was the most intense experience yet.

Perhaps it was because he'd spent so much time this past year with his now fifteen-month-old niece and four-year-old nephew. Or maybe it had something to do with finally, at age twenty-nine, having finished his training and taken his place as a full-fledged specialist.

Turning away, he stripped off his gloves and picked up his clipboard to finish his notes. Then, smiling, Quent paced through the dimly lit nursery, saying hello to babies he'd checked in the past day or two. He would see them again when their parents brought them for regular care at the Well-Baby Clinic in an adjacent building, where he spent most of his hours.

Before leaving the nursery, he removed his white coverall and stuffed it into a laundry container to be sterilized. A nurse, Sue Anne, greeted him with a flare of interest on her face.

Quent wasn't sure why he didn't invite her to join him for dinner, since it was almost five o'clock on a Friday night. She was pretty and friendly, and, until recently, he'd enjoyed playing the field. These days, though, he'd lost interest in spending time with anyone except his best buddy.

Having a woman, even a colleague like psychologist Amy Ravenna, as his best buddy was unusual, he supposed. Still, they'd started attending ball games and playing sports together as if it were the most natural thing in the world, and going with the flow suited Quent.

Speak of the devil, when he emerged from the nursery, there she stood, Amy in the flesh, gazing through the window at the babies. Among the usual scattering of cooing grandparents, aunts and uncles, her tall, slim figure stood out.

In profile to him, Amy studied first one baby, then another. As the staff psychologist, she must be treating the parents of one or more infants, Quent figured. Checking out the newborns apparently figured into her counseling strategy, although he could have sworn he saw wistfulness in her expression.

He'd never met anyone with such an intriguing mixture of professionalism and tomboy enthusiasm. It amused him to see how, this late in the day, her black French braid was beginning to unravel behind her tailored suit jacket.

"Hey," he said.

Startled, Amy swung around. "Oh! Hi, Quent." He noticed, as he did every time he saw her, how stunning she was, with her high cheekbones and lively dark eyes, and how utterly unaware she was of it. No wonder she had to fend men off with a stick.

"What brings you here?" With a teasing note, he added, "Coming to see me, I hope."

"As a matter of fact, yes. Before I left for the day, I wanted to ask you about the rain," she said.

"It's raining?" Mid-November was well into the southern California rainy season, but it had been only partly cloudy earlier this afternoon.

"Not yet. It's in the forecast for tomorrow. We're supposed to catch the tail of a hurricane that's lingering down off Mexico," Amy said. "Do you want to cancel our plans?"

"I'm not afraid of a little water. Are you?" He already knew the answer, but challenging each other was part of the fun.

Soon after he'd arrived in Serene Beach, he'd run into Amy at the sports-oriented Paris Bar and recognized her as a colleague. That first night, they'd battled each other at video games until their eyes crossed from overuse. Soon they were jogging together, watching ball games and simply hanging out after work, with no strings attached. Amy was never flirtatious as other women were.

At first, that had been a relief. Lately, it had occurred to Quent that maybe, being four years older than him and accustomed to more sophisticated men, she considered him too young for anything more involved than going to the movies. He might surprise her one of these days.

"Afraid of water? Certainly not." She sniffed in feigned indignation. "The fact is, I figured you might wimp out on me. It's going to be hard enough jogging in the sand when you're not used to it, without having to deal with a downpour, too."

"If you can handle sand, so can I." He couldn't resist adding, "I'll probably run you ragged."

"I'll bet you won't." The way Amy lifted her chin reminded him that she'd held her own in a household with three brothers.

"You're on for tomorrow," he said.

"My place. Three o'clock."

"I'll be there." He was looking forward to it.

AMY JOGGED in place, waiting for the light at Pacific Coast Highway to change. The rain was so heavy, she could hardly see the signal.

"I thought you could handle anything," Quent challenged. Beside her, he stood grinning cockily, not seeming to mind that the downpour had flattened his thick blond hair and made his T-shirt cling like a second skin to his sculpted chest.

"So I lied," she said, tearing her gaze away from his muscular build.

Everything was fine as long as they kept things on a buddy level. Amy would rather shrivel up and get rinsed down the drain than let Quent know that she found him just as irresistible as did all the nurses and receptionists who gossiped about him at work.

He assumed, because she encouraged him to, that Amy knew the ropes. She made frequent, joking references to her active social life and many admirers because that was a lot more comfortable than letting him, or anyone other than her closest friends, know the truth.

She was a tomboy who rarely dated. Always had been and, like it or not, probably always would be.

Amy wished she knew how to be more feminine, but, until she'd met Quent, she hadn't had a good enough reason to venture outside her comfort zone. Now she didn't know where to start. Maybe, with him, it was too late.

At one point this afternoon, they'd drifted a short distance apart while jogging. The next thing she knew, a lushly built woman in tight exercise shorts and a halter top had fallen into step with Quent and was inviting him home for a drink.

The woman hadn't even known his name! Where did she get the nerve? Or the courage?

Amy wished she knew how to flirt so easily. She wished she were smaller and daintier with a large bust and full lips.

On the other hand, Quent hadn't accepted the offer, had he?

The light changed. "Go!" Amy said, and shot forward.

Although she'd been faster off the curb, Quent's long stride caught her up by the time they'd crossed the six lanes. With her peripheral vision, Amy could see the hard muscles pumping in his thighs and buttocks as he passed her.

Determined not to be left behind, she put on a burst of speed and moved ahead. Growing up in a family of men, she'd learned to push herself to the limit.

Quent made no effort to reclaim the lead. He seemed content to match her pace as they traversed the funky neighborhood, whose narrow streets and pocket-sized dwellings belied its exorbitant real-estate prices.

Living near the beach wasn't cheap. Amy was grateful that she'd managed to find a condo that suited her budget.

A quarter mile farther on, they arrived breathless at her complex. The condos were two stories high except for hers, at one end. Due to the lay of the land, if it had had more than one story, it would have blocked the view from an expensive home located behind it. Serene Beach had an ordinance protecting properties' views.

As the two of them hurried along the walkway, rain streamed into the unoccupied swimming pool and a couple of palm trees swayed in the stiffening wind. This was turning into a gale.

Amy unlocked her door. "Coming in?"

She wasn't sure what she hoped he'd say. They usually met in neutral places, only entering her condo for a game of darts or to grab a beer from the fridge. Partly by choice, she hadn't visited Quent's apartment at all.

There was no sense in tormenting yourself with what you couldn't have. Or, more accurately, with what you doubted you could handle.

"That's the best invitation I've had all day." With a grin, he waited for her to enter, then followed her in.

There was no turning back now. Not that she expected anything much to happen.

While Quent waited, dripping, in the tiled entryway, Amy retrieved a couple of towels from the bathroom and tossed him one.

"Great," Quent said, drying his face. "This will greatly lessen our risk of hypothermia."

"Spoken like a doctor."

"I'm not entirely kidding. I can hear your teeth chattering," he said.

Okay, so she was shivering in her running clothes. Big deal. "I'll be fine as soon as I make coffee." Amy pulled off her sodden shoes and dropped them in a corner. "No, wait. I'm out."

"You're out of coffee?" Quent said. "That's un-American."

"I think I've got a bag of microwave popcorn left."

"Just one?"

"I didn't make it to the supermarket this week." Amy swiped the towel across her legs.

When Amy was twelve, her mother had run off with another man, and she hadn't wanted to become a substitute housekeeper for her brothers and her father, a chiropractor. As a result, she'd avoided cooking and shopping as much as possible.

Unfortunately, her youthful habits had become ingrained. Amy had developed such a mental block that, even as an adult, she procrastinated about any kind of shopping. If her friends Natalie and Heather hadn't pushed her to find furnishings for her condo, she might still be sleeping on a futon.

"I'll make the popcorn. You go change." Quent caught her shoulders and steered her toward the bedrooms.

Amy wasn't sure which pleased her most, his touch or the fact that he was taking care of her. Not that it meant anything. He was her buddy, that was all.

"Need a dry sweatshirt?" she asked. His thin running shorts looked like the type to dry quickly and, besides, she definitely didn't have anything that would fit him there.

"Sure," he said. "As long as it doesn't say 49ers on it."

"I hope you don't think I would sully my house with a Chargers sweatshirt!" Amy retorted.

They both claimed fierce allegiance to their home teams. She wasn't sure either of them really meant it, and, since Serene Beach was located between the two teams' territories, their rivalry never amounted to more than a little teasing.

Come baseball season, no doubt they'd simply switch the names of the teams and continue their rivalry. Or, more likely, by then Quent would have found himself a girlfriend and wouldn't have time to kid around with her. Amy's throat tightened at the prospect.

In a bedroom that featured sports posters above a

light-oak bed and bureau, she stripped off her soaked garments. After a moment's debate, she pulled on a forest-green sweater over a pair of jeans and brushed her long black hair out of its ponytail. She added a touch of lipstick, which was as much makeup as she usually wore.

Amy regarded herself in the small mirror above the dresser. Darn, she couldn't see the whole picture. Come to think of it, she didn't own a full-length mirror, because she so rarely needed one.

What was she fussing about anyway? she asked herself grumpily. It wasn't as if Quent was going to suddenly notice she was a girl. Or as if she wanted him to, given that he'd made it clear when they'd first met that he was bent on sowing his wild oats after years of grinding away at his medical studies. The last thing Amy needed was to lose her heart to a man who was only looking for a good time.

Remembering her promise to provide him with warm clothing, she prowled through the closet. From the back, she lifted out a bright-pink sweatshirt bearing the image of a black cat. Her friend Natalie Winford, who was soon to become the bride of the clinic's administrator, had bought it for her at the nearby Black Cat Café as an impulsive gift.

Pulling it off the hanger, Amy scooted past the second bedroom, which served as a home office, and the third one, which was empty. The combination living-dining room had the usual assortment of furniture, thanks to her friends' supervision, but Amy had augmented the decor with a few touches of her own.

There was, for instance, the electronic dartboard on one wall. Also, a video-game system dominated the dining table. To Amy, they made the place feel like home.

There was no sign of Quent. Judging by the mouth-watering scent, he'd kept his promise to make popcorn.

She found him in the kitchen, larger than life and twice as sexy, leaning against the counter. When Quent wasn't working or otherwise active, he always seemed to be leaning on something, Amy mused.

The first time she'd seen him, he'd been holding up one wall of the hallway between her counseling office and the Well-Baby Clinic. She had the same reaction now that she'd had then: a racing heartbeat and a melting sensation in her core.

Now, as then, she did her best to ignore it.

"I'm glad to see what a gourmet cook you are," Quent joked, nodding toward the take-out sacks stuffed in the wastebasket.

"Huh. Anybody can whip up a chicken cordon bleu." Amy indicated a refrigerator magnet displaying the phone number of a local pizza parlor. "I'm famous for devising the most inventive combinations this side of Italy. Ever try pineapple, anchovies and onions?"

"I think I treated a kid for eating one of those last week," Quent said. "By the way, I made the mistake of opening your fridge and nearly got sucked into the void."

"You're just mad because I'm out of beer."

"That, too." He removed the bag of popcorn from the microwave and replaced it with two mugs of water. Judging by the box of hot chocolate mix sitting nearby, Amy guessed she was in for a treat.

A thrumming noise drew her attention to the window. "What a torrent! It's only rained this hard once or twice since I moved in." She'd come to Serene Beach four years ago, after counseling patients at a low-cost clinic in Fresno.

"We could light a fire in the fireplace," Quent said.

A crackling blaze, hot chocolate, the man of her dreams taking her in his arms... Abruptly, Amy's idyll vanished and she came down to earth. Or, more accurately, down to hearth.

"I don't have a fireplace," she said. "How about a portable heater?"

"Does it glow when it gets hot?" Quent asked.

She nodded.

"That'll do." He indicated the garment tucked under her arm. "What's that?"

"Catch." She tossed him the pink sweatshirt. "As I promised."

He held it up. "Not really my color."

"Pink looks good on blondes," Amy said.

"In that case, how can I refuse?" He shrugged off his clinging wet shirt, gave his powerful chest a swipe from his towel, and reached for the sweatshirt.

Her kingdom for a camera, Amy thought. She wanted to stroke him so much her palms itched. It was almost an ache, this need to run her hands along that rippling bare skin and feel the masculine hardness.

She didn't dare risk changing their relationship that way. Either Quent would start to feel uncomfortable around her or he'd add her to his collection of conquests. Either way, it would spell the end of their good times.

He yanked the sweatshirt into place. Although loose on Amy, it clung to him. "Not bad," he said. "You loan this to all your boyfriends?"

"Only the blond ones," she said.

"I hope you wash it in between." The microwave bell rang, summoning Quent.

"Usually. If I remember. I mean, they come and go so fast, who can keep track?"

She didn't like misleading him, even as a joke, but if Quent discovered how little experience she had, the man would laugh. Amy couldn't bear to be teased about the fact that she'd reached her third decade still a virgin, and not entirely by choice. Above all, she didn't want Quent to be the man to whom she finally gave herself, because it would mean so much more to her than it possibly could to him.

Someday, Amy hoped to find a gentle, undemanding guy who would love and treasure her. The problem was that when she did meet men of that description, she felt a big fat nothing toward them. Certainly not the scary, exhilarating sense of riding a roller coaster that hit her every time she imagined Quent's mouth covering hers, his body pressing her down…

"Is it something I said?" He stood there holding out a steaming mug of cocoa. "Or are you ignoring me on purpose?"

"I was remembering the last macho hunk who wore that sweatshirt," Amy invented.

"I could wipe up the floor with him."

"Oh, yeah? He was a wrestler."

"Professionally?" he asked.

"Just with me," she said. "I won, by the way. Pinned him best two out of three. Come to think of it, we never got to three."

Carrying the popcorn, Quent led the way into the living room. "Maybe we should try that."

"I wouldn't want to hurt you," she said.

"Hurt me? You didn't take a close enough look at my muscles while I had my shirt off," he shot back. "Care for me to strip again?"

With all my heart. "I'll pass," Amy said. "Hang on."

She set aside her mug and dug through the front closet for the portable heater. She found it behind her ski poles and Boogie board.

Set up in front of the couch and plugged into an extension cord, it radiated a luxurious circle of warmth. Amy and Quent sank onto the sofa to enjoy it.

For some reason, they kept sliding to the middle. She tried not to react when his knee nudged hers or to the brush of his shoulder as he raised his mug to drink. But she couldn't help it.

"I like your hair loose that way." Quent's voice sounded hoarse.

"It won't dry in a ponytail so I shook it out." She couldn't meet his eyes, not sitting this close. They'd practically be kissing.

Overhead, a gust of wind hit the roof. Instinctively, she shifted closer to Quent, as if he could protect her from the storm.

Their hands met when they reached into the popcorn bag at the same time. Amy's skin prickled.

"Next time I'll stock up on supplies so we can each have our own," she said.

"I prefer it this way," Quent murmured.

She stopped trying to deny the heat deep inside her, the tingling in her lips, the inability to think of anything except Quent's broad chest. She simply had to find an excuse to touch him, just once.

"Are you sure that sweatshirt isn't too tight?" She ran her hand across his shoulders. "It looks snug."

"I can't tell you what that does to a guy." He set his mug beside Amy's on the coffee table and clasped her waist. "You're going to slug me for this, but I can't resist."

Amy's mind went white. Time slowed, and the universe filled with the slow, inevitable descent of Quent's mouth onto hers.

Her lips parted to welcome him. Despite its tenderness, the kiss jolted her. She swayed toward him until her breasts grazed his chest.

His palms caressed her hips, bringing her closer, then raised trails of sparkles as he stroked up her rib cage. She ought to draw back. Ought to, but couldn't.

Amy played her hands along Quent's back, down to that incredibly tight masculine butt. She might never get this chance again, she thought dazedly.

When his tongue explored the corners of her lips, she teased it with light nips that intensified his probing. At the same time, wonder of wonders, his strong, skilled hands slid beneath the waistline of her sweater and smoothed upwards to the swell of her breasts.

She wore only a thin sports bra, a fact that he discovered rapidly. His hands covered the small nubs, arousing white-hot flames that licked through her body.

Was he simply acting like a guy, responding unthinkingly to whatever woman he found himself with? Amy didn't know, and didn't want to know. She'd never felt such powerful sensations before.

"Amazing." Quent drew his head back. "I should have known you'd be…you'd be…"

Whatever he meant to say, Amy was never to learn, because at that moment a huge crash shook the room. It felt as if a bomb had gone off.

She was too shocked to move until cold water blasted her face and tiny pieces of something spattered across her hand. "What on earth?"

With an oath, Quent pulled her away from the couch. "We'd better turn off the power before something catches fire." He reached down and unplugged the heater. "That's for good measure."

There were pieces of white ceiling plaster clinging to her sweater, Amy realized. Her brain still struggled to accept what had happened, but by the time they reached the doorway en route to the fuse box, the truth dawned.

She'd finally kissed the man of her dreams, and the roof had caved in.

Chapter Two

"That's one heckuva palm tree," said the fireman, studying the wreckage from the rain-drenched parking lot.

The tree had fallen straight across Amy's roof, smashing shingles and the gutter. The fire-team members, their bright yellow slickers deflecting the downpour, had thrown a tarp over the roof to protect the contents from further damage, but it was clear the place would be unlivable for some time to come.

"How big do you make it?" Quent asked. "Twenty, thirty feet?"

"Hard to tell. You'll need to get a private contractor out here to cut it up and haul it away, and you'll need to board over that hole it made. I'd suggest you contact a roofer as soon as possible." The man turned to talk to another firefighter.

The sheeting rain and stormy late-afternoon darkness diffused the lights of the rescue vehicles. Their flashing reds and haloed whites reflected eerily off the blacktop.

Holding the umbrella a neighbor had loaned them, Quent strolled to the overhang where Amy stood surveying the mess. "You wouldn't happen to know a good roofer, would you?" he asked.

"The condo association will take care of it," she said. "I already called the manager." Somehow, he saw, she'd managed to snag her purse and cell phone on their way out of the unit. "They're the ones who carry our insurance and maintain the common roof."

"We've been complaining about that tree for years," grumbled the middle-aged woman who'd given Quent the umbrella. "I'm glad nobody got hurt."

"I'm going to ask the battalion chief if it's safe to go in and fetch some of my clothes." Amy took the umbrella. "My laptop, too, and some case files I brought home."

"I'll talk to him." Quent swiveled toward the firemen.

"It's my condo. Besides, those guys have been taking funny looks at your sweatshirt," she said.

"Huh?" He glanced down in surprise. Darn, he'd forgotten about the pink top and the feminine-looking cat.

"I can handle the situation," Amy said. "Why don't you just stand here and look pretty?"

"Why not? I'm so good at it," he shot back. Her answering grin told him she'd enjoyed the quip.

Despite his remark, Quent would have preferred to take care of business himself, but Amy had already crossed the pavement. Her slim figure managed to be authoritative and sweetly appealing at the same time as she put her case to the man in the yellow slicker.

"Tell Amy to keep the umbrella as long as she needs it," said the neighbor, and went inside.

Quent stuck his hands in his pockets to keep from obeying his instincts to charge out there and protect Amy. It was obvious she didn't need his help.

She stood her ground, speaking calmly as the chief

listened. A younger fireman, working nearby, kept glancing at her with unconcealed interest. If that guy came any closer, Quent was going to intervene.

It came as a relief when the younger man moved away. Besides, the guy looked too callow for Amy.

Quent hoped he hadn't annoyed her by grabbing her that way on the couch. After holding himself in check all these weeks, he'd seized his chance so abruptly he hadn't shown much subtlety.

Maybe it was a good thing they'd been interrupted. Going to bed with Amy would be fabulous, but he wasn't sure how they could strike the right balance. Relationships, in his experience, had a way of careening out of control.

Several years ago, Quent had nearly become engaged to a graduate student in business. The closer he and his girlfriend grew, however, the more they'd quarreled.

She'd resented his long hours at the hospital, while he'd experienced a spurt of jealousy when he saw her studying with a male friend. Their friendship had degenerated into mistrust and tension that all his efforts had failed to dispel. Soon they'd broken up and gone their own ways.

He didn't want anything like that to happen with Amy. He didn't want to lose her, and he knew their relationship would change irrevocably once they became intimate. Yet there'd been a fierceness to her response that stirred him profoundly. The things she could teach him...

He swallowed hard and tried to turn his thoughts to something unpleasant to cool his ardor. Foul-tasting medicine. Tetanus shots. Dr. Fingger, the interim head of the Well-Baby Clinic, wearing his customary prune-sucking expression of disapproval.

The tactic failed, to Quent's dismay. He knew perfectly well that his cutoffs didn't hide much of anything. He preferred not to think of Amy's pals chuckling if she described his awkward groping on the couch, followed by his obvious physical arousal as he stood watching her in the rain like some lustful tomcat.

Oh, heck, Amy wasn't the kind of woman to make fun of him to others. At least, Quent didn't think so, but the image of her friends' mirth succeeded where his discouraging thoughts had failed, and his body came under control.

Amy returned a moment later. "They believe the place is structurally safe but they have to err on the side of caution," she said. "They're going to allow me inside for ten minutes. Can you believe that? Ten minutes to collect my gear for who knows how long!"

"Let me help," he said.

"Great! I'd appreciate it." She led the way to the wide-open front door. "We're ready," she told the battalion chief.

He nodded. "Go on in."

The two of them hurried into a living room that resembled a war zone. It was too bad one lousy tree could do so much damage.

The other rooms appeared undamaged. With her usual efficiency, Amy handed Quent a suitcase from the hall closet.

"I'm going to get the papers and laptop out of my office," she said. "Grab my clothes out of the bedroom, will you? Business suits, jeans and blouses are in the closet. My underwear's in the top drawer of the bureau and my nightgowns are in the middle."

"You want me to handle your—?" He stopped, remembering that they had only ten minutes and he was wasting time. Her approach made sense, since he'd have no idea what papers to take or where to find them in her office. "Okay."

She vanished through a doorway to the right. The other bedroom on that side was empty, so Quent turned left.

The first thing that struck him was Amy's fresh floral scent. The second thing were the framed posters of ice skaters and gymnasts. He was surprised not to see one of the 49ers, and realized she must not be as big a fan as she claimed.

After plopping the suitcase on the bed, he retrieved some clothes from their hangers. There wasn't time to fold them neatly. Suits, jeans and blouses all got rolled up and stuffed inside.

Although he knew they were pressed for time, Quent hesitated before opening the bureau drawers. He didn't like invading Amy's privacy. Even with his girlfriend, his only contact with her lingerie and lace nighties had been removing them in a hurry.

He yanked on the center drawer first and took out a folded nightgown. The silky fabric flowed across his hands like warm water. Draped on Amy's body, it must reveal every curve and inlet, he thought, and hurriedly stuffed it into the suitcase.

Quent braved the top drawer. Panties and bras were stuffed together, entangled with pantyhose. The jumble reminded him of his own sock drawer.

Try as he might, he couldn't suppress an image of Amy wearing this stuff and peeling it off in front of him. With her experience, she'd probably perfected the art of the striptease.

"Hey!" the subject of his yearnings called from the

hallway. "They're calling for us to come out. You ready?"

"I'll be right there!" Quent grabbed a handful of underwear, shoved it into the suitcase and clicked it shut.

They scurried out together. Amy lugged a satchel full of papers plus her laptop and the umbrella. "I'm glad they let me in there. I kept thinking of other things I need. Did you get everything?"

"You bet," Quent said. "If I ever need a job as a ladies' maid, you can give me a reference."

"You did take some shoes, didn't you?" she asked.

"Shoes?"

"You know, the things to go on my feet?" Amy groaned as they emerged into the blustery day. "Oh, well, I suppose it's my fault for forgetting to mention it."

The firemen refused to let them back in. "The building inspector called and said to keep the premises vacated until he makes sure it's safe," the battalion chief told them. "He won't be able to get here before Monday."

"I'll survive," Amy said. "At least I've got my credit cards."

"I'll pay you back for the shoes," Quent said.

"You will not. I can always use a new pair."

She left the place open, after the chief promised to lock up personally when his crew was finished and give the key to her neighbor. Even under the eaves, the air hung heavy with moisture, and Quent knew they both needed to get dry.

In the parking lot, he got a bright idea. Well, maybe not totally bright, if he'd given himself time to think about it, but right now Quent's brain couldn't stretch beyond the need to get Amy alone and resume the activity that had been so rudely interrupted.

"You can stay with me," he said.

She handed him the umbrella and, waving aside his attempt to help, began stowing things in the trunk of her sporty sedan, which she'd moved out of her carport because it, too, was damaged. "You're inviting me to move in with you till my roof gets fixed?"

"Why not?" That was one of Quent's mottos.

"Because…" Amy pushed back a strand of black hair that had draped itself across her cheek. Quent fought down the urge to reach out and stroke that tantalizing wisp. "We're friends. If I move in with you, stuff will happen, and then we'll both get self-conscious about it and we might not be friends anymore."

"Sure we will." He had a sneaking suspicion she was right, but it didn't pay to think too far in advance, because you never knew what the future would bring. "Life's too short to deny yourself."

"You really believe that?"

Quent shifted the umbrella, trying to keep them both dry. Rain tickled the back of his neck. "Sure I do."

"Don't you ever worry about consequences?"

"Not if I can help it." At least, that had been his attitude until last year, when his niece and nephew were orphaned. Even since then, however, he preferred not to dwell on things he couldn't control.

Amy shook her head. "Whatever works for you. Anyway, thanks for the offer, but my aunt lives a couple of miles away. I'm hoping she'll take me in."

A mixture of disappointment and relief welled up in Quent. Sure, he wanted to take Amy home and ravish her. He'd been fantasizing about it for weeks.

But underneath her gung-ho exterior, he knew Amy

was complicated. Around her, he sometimes caught himself thinking about things he was in no way ready for, like a long-term relationship.

"You're sure?" he said.

"Positive." She reached out and ruffled his hair. "See you at work on Monday."

"You bet."

He handed her the umbrella and waited until she pulled out of the parking lot before taking refuge in his SUV. Quent debated whether to stay and keep an eye on her unit until the condo association got workmen out here. Considering that it was nearly dusk on a Saturday, however, he might have a very long wait. If Amy wasn't worried about security, she probably knew best, he decided, and pulled away.

He negotiated the side streets to Pacific Coast Highway and swung north onto Serene Boulevard, which ran uphill toward the inland mesa area where he lived. Partially blocked by fallen palm fronds and other wind-blown debris, traffic inched up a steep incline toward the bluffs that separated the beach area from the mesa.

Quent was passing Serene Park, a green expanse with a great view of the ocean, when one of his contact lenses began to smart. It was a sharp, intense itch, as if a grain of sand had worked its way under there. Concerned about driving with such a distraction, he pulled into the deserted park and stopped.

There was no sense trying to fix things under these circumstances, so Quent popped out both lenses. He replaced them with a pair of glasses from the glove compartment.

Water gusted across the windshield and drummed on the roof. The SUV swayed in a burst of wind. Even the tail of a hurricane could pack a lot of force, he mused, and decided to wait awhile before resuming his journey along the clogged street. Maybe this downpour would let up.

Only now, sitting quietly with rain pounding outside, did Quent become aware of the tautness in his body. It wasn't the pleasurable sexual tension he'd felt earlier with Amy, but an intermittent uneasiness that had dogged him for the past year.

He realized he was having a delayed reaction to the crash of the tree breaking through the roof. It had brought back with vivid clarity the moment when he'd awakened in darkness to the jarring ring of the phone. He'd still been living in San Diego, where he'd grown up, and had been finishing his neonatology residency.

For a disoriented moment, he'd figured one of his roommates would grab the phone. When neither answered, he'd remembered they were both working the night shift, so he'd answered.

He could still hear his father's voice, almost toneless with shock. "They're dead," he'd said. "I should have seen it coming. Why did Jeffrey let her drive?"

Quent's first reaction had been confusion. "What do you mean, they're dead? Who's dead?"

"Everyone," Bruce Ladd had growled. "All of them. Except the kids."

Until that moment, the demands of studying and working combined with his own playful nature had kept Quent from paying much attention to his family's problems. He'd assumed the people he loved would always be around, always be fine, always be able to manage.

He knew that his mother, Alice, drank too much, and that his father responded by withdrawing emotionally. He'd never understood why his older brother Jeffrey refused to acknowledge the seriousness of Alice's drinking, but then, Quent had tried to persuade her to seek help and knew how futile that was.

That night changed everything, too late. He hadn't known, at a gut emotional level, that the people you loved could suddenly be snatched away from you. And he'd never imagined the abyss that would open up inside.

At the hospital, he learned that Jeffrey, Jeffrey's wife Paula, their infant daughter and young son had gone with Alice to a friend's barbecue in the countryside. Quent's father, Bruce, had declined, because he had brought home overflow work from his law practice.

At the barbecue, liquor flowed. Afterwards, even though Jeffrey must have known Alice had been drinking, he'd allowed her to take the wheel of her car. It was, sadly, typical "enabling" behavior.

Driving too fast at night, she'd swerved to avoid hitting the back of a slow-moving semi truck. The car had veered off a small bridge and into a swollen creek.

All three adults were killed. The truck driver and a passerby had managed to unstrap the children and bring them to safety, but they'd been unable to save the others.

In the months that followed, Quent had steered his father into treatment for depression while struggling with his own sense of helplessness and regret. He'd also done his best to help the children get settled.

At the time, Quent had been working rotating shifts that made parenting an infant and a preschooler impossible. Since his father was in no condition to raise them and Paula's mother suffered from severe arthritis, Paula's sister Lucy had become their guardian.

Single and a bit flaky, she was a good sport, but he wondered now if she'd realized what she was taking on.

Although Quent had visited frequently while he lived in San Diego, he had to be on call most weekends since moving to Orange County and it was hard to find time to make the three-hour round-trip drive.

As another blast of rain hit the glass, he recalled with a guilty twinge that he hadn't talked to his niece and nephew in several weeks. The last time had been when Lucy called to thank him for some gifts he'd sent Tara and Greg.

He took out his cell phone and dialed.

"Hello? Enlighten me." It was Lucy, who, even at twenty-six, sometimes talked like a teenager. During the week, she was an assistant department manager at a large insurance company that provided child care. On the weekends, her passion was long-distance running.

"It's Quent. How's the weather down there?"

"Miserable, which is why I'm working out indoors." In the background, he heard the squeak of her treadmill. "Man, I hate this humidity. If I wanted humidity, I'd move to Florida."

"How're the kids?"

"Going crazy from being cooped up. Hang on." A moment later, she put Greg on the phone.

Sounding grown-up for a four-year-old, he filled Quent in on his day-care group's adventures in making something called stone soup. Apparently it included numerous ingredients, although no actual stones.

"We heard this story about it. The man said he could make soup from a stone," Greg explained. "He talked this old lady into giving him stuff to make it taste better. You know, like noodles and onions."

"Very clever," Quent said.

Next, Tara babbled away happily, interposing a few recognizable words with her baby talk. Child development fascinated Quent. He'd studied the physical and emotional facts of childhood, but it was much more striking to observe them outside a clinical setting, especially when you cared so much about the youngsters.

He wondered if Amy liked kids. As a counselor who spent her life helping people, surely she did, and she'd shown a marked interest in the newborns yesterday. Maybe someday she'd enjoy meeting Tara and Greg.

"I'll come see you soon," Quent promised before saying goodbye to each child in turn.

"They miss you," Lucy said. She didn't include herself. The two of them had been practically strangers until the tragedy and, although they got along fine, had little in common apart from the children.

"How're you doing?" he asked.

"Okay. I'm not much of a mother type but we muddle along. Thank goodness they like macaroni and cheese," she said.

"I'd like to come visit soon. When would be convenient?"

"I'm not sure. We've got a lot of changes at work and I've had to put in some extra hours," Lucy said. "I'll give you a call, okay?"

"Thanks."

After he rang off, Quent was glad to see the rain slackening. It was growing dark, turning from daytime into Saturday night. After years of overwork, he loved to party, and rarely got the chance. Now where had he put that flier?

He dug through a handful of papers on the passenger seat. There was a staff memo from Dr. Fingger about the Thanksgiving holiday schedule, filled with exhortations not to be late or ask for changes. The guy really needed to loosen up.

Beneath it lay a reminder about the annual pre-Christmas soiree hosted by the Doctors Circle administrator, Patrick Barr, which this year was going to double as his wedding reception. It made sense to Quent that the guy was getting maximum bang for the buck.

Here it was! He pulled out the flier he'd been handed by Rob Sentinel, a new obstetrician at the clinic. Rob was hosting a bring-your-own bottle party tonight, promising loud music, lousy food and nowhere near enough chairs. Perfect!

It would be more fun if Amy could go, but he suspected she'd be busy settling in at her aunt's. Well, the two of them weren't joined at the hip.

After the grind of medical school, Quent had sworn to take it easy when he got the chance. He'd had less time for fun than he expected during his residencies, and now he seized every opportunity to blow off steam.

He put the SUV into gear and headed to a convenience store. He'd better pick up some taco chips and spray cheese in case Rob ran short. It wasn't fair to let one guy shoulder the whole work of staging a party by himself.

Chapter Three

Amy was almost asleep when the cell phone rang on her bedside table. Thinking it might be one of her clients, she shook off her daze as she grabbed it. "Amy Ravenna," she said.

"Quentin Ladd," came the response. He sounded utterly mellow. The background noise of conversation and music gave her a clue why.

Amy checked the clock. Nearly midnight. "You went to that party of Rob Sentinel's, didn't you?" She tried to quell a spurt of jealousy that came from knowing plenty of single nurses must be present.

"Bingo," he said.

"And you've had a few beers."

"Two," he said. "I never have more than two." He made a point of never drinking to excess.

"Is something wrong?" she asked sleepily, and hoped the ringing phone hadn't disturbed her aunt Mary or seventeen-year-old cousin Kitty, who'd both gone to bed an hour ago.

"Yes," Quent said. "You're not here."

Warmth seeped through Amy. "I thought of going, but Aunt Mary and I were figuring out what to fix for Thanksgiving." It was only a few days away.

"Throw on some clothes and come join me."

She'd rather he took off his clothes and joined *her.* Uh-oh. She hadn't said that aloud, had she? "I'd better not," Amy said. "I'm tired and it's raining."

"It's stopped. Besides, we have some unfinished business." His tone wasn't exactly suggestive, and he certainly wasn't applying pressure. It was more of an open invitation, leaving the decision to her.

Amy knew how she had to respond. "It's best left unfinished."

"We'll see." A couple of short breaths revealed that he was yawning.

"You're tired," she said. "Go home."

"I needed somebody to tell me that," Quent admitted. "I hope I'm not getting too old to party hearty anymore."

"You're nearly thirty."

"Ouch!"

"A little maturity will look good on you," she said.

"That's encouraging." In the background, someone turned up the volume. Nearly shouting, Quent added, "That could damage my hearing!"

"You're definitely too old for that scene," Amy said. "Go put on your tasseled nightcap and heat a water bottle for your tootsies. I'll see you on Monday."

"Count on it," he said.

After ringing off, Amy couldn't resist picturing what might have happened if she'd accepted his invitation. They'd have ended up alone at his apartment, stroking each other, kissing, sinking onto the couch with no one to interfere and no inconvenient tree to collapse on top of them....

She pushed the image away and picked up a psychology journal from the bedside table. It was half an hour before her eyes drifted shut again.

SHOES. Who knew they could be such a problem?

Amy's size must have been wildly popular, because on Sunday her favorite department store was out of stock in all the pumps that appealed to her.

She didn't blame Quent. She hadn't mentioned packing her shoes, although heaven knew what the guy had been thinking.

Uh, wait. She did know. He'd been thinking about their hot-and-heavy madness on the couch. What else was a twenty-something guy supposed to think about?

Not to mention a thirty-something woman.

Amy tried not to survey the men as she raced down the mall to a specialty shoe store. She didn't want to compare their butts—unfavorably—to Quent's, or to notice how their hair lacked the wild springiness of his.

She was not going to view him as a sex object. He was her buddy and her respected colleague. And way too eager to make love to the woman of the world he assumed her to be.

If only they had met in an alternate reality where mindless fun carried no consequences, they could indulge themselves and go right on being friends and co-workers. If that were true, her images from last night would already have become a sizzling reality.

Giving herself a mental slap, Amy entered the store and picked out several pairs of pumps. At last, she found a pair that fit and finished paying barely in time to meet her two closest friends for their appointment at the bridal shop.

Natalie Winford, a blond divorcée with a wicked sense of humor, was getting married in two weeks to the administrator of Doctors Circle. A pediatrician who'd left his practice to work full-time as director, Patrick was the son of the clinic's late founder.

Natalie, his longtime secretary, had nursed her secret love for years until the two of them got carried away one night after a party to raise money for the center's Endowment Fund. Now here she was, due to deliver a baby next May and deliriously happy after discovering that Patrick had been secretly in love with her, too.

Several weeks earlier, the attendants had picked out their turquoise bridesmaids' gowns along with matching hats. The problem, once again, was the shoes.

"I'm sorry," the store proprietor said, holding up a pair of emerald pumps. "They came out the wrong color. I called you as soon as I saw them."

"Dye another batch," Natalie said promptly.

"The company we use is backlogged, and so is everyone else," the woman said. "I'm terribly sorry. I've called all over Orange and Los Angeles counties and I haven't had any luck."

"We could wear white shoes," suggested their friend Heather Rourke, an obstetrician who was on two months' leave for personal reasons. "Or would we be stepping on the bride's toes?"

"If that was an intentional pun, I'm going to stick you with a diaper pin," Amy said.

Heather laughed. "I don't think they make diaper pins anymore. Everything's got Velcro or tape."

"You should know."

"Just call me Diaper Lady!"

The beautiful redhead had recently admitted to her two closest friends, after swearing them to secrecy, that she'd given up a baby for adoption while in her teens. Following the deaths of the adoptive parents, her daughter Olive had contacted her, and they'd become close. Then Olive became pregnant.

Heather had taken leave to coach her daughter through childbirth while Olive's fiancé served overseas in the marines. Now the new mother and baby Ginger were staying with Grandma, which seemed to Amy an absurd title for such a young-looking thirty-six-year-old. No one else at the center knew anything about the situation, and Heather, who prized her privacy, intended to keep it that way.

"I wish my sister hadn't had to work today so you could all pick out your shoes," Natalie said. "We're getting awfully close to the wedding."

"Candy doesn't have to wear the same shoes we do," Heather pointed out. "She's the maid of honor."

"I don't see why any of our shoes have to match," Amy said. "Who's going to notice? We'll look weird enough as it is, wearing turquoise at the reception. I assume the Barr mansion will be decked out in red and green as usual."

Every year, Patrick hosted the Doctors Circle staff and supporters at a holiday party the first week in December. Since he and Natalie had become engaged at the end of October, they'd had such a short time to prepare that they'd decided to let the annual event do double duty.

"I thought about having a Christmas-themed wedding," Nat admitted. "But red is too far out and I couldn't stick you guys with bright green dresses."

"Thanks, more than you'll ever know," Amy said.

She couldn't imagine how brides kept track of all the details and conventions, anyway. If she ever got married, she'd have to elope, because otherwise she would make a whole series of embarrassing faux pas.

"I'm glad you picked turquoise and silver," Heather said. "The church will be beautiful."

"Silver! That's it!" Although Amy had the fashion sense of a sea slug, she knew she'd hit on something this time. "Last year at Patrick's Christmas reception, there were silver bows on the staircase. If we wear silver shoes, they'll work at the wedding *and* the reception."

"Silver would be lovely," Natalie agreed.

"I don't suppose you have any silver shoes on hand, do you?" Heather asked the proprietor.

"I'm afraid not."

They spent the rest of the afternoon traipsing around the mall, and found two attractive styles of silver sandals that would look fine side by side. Heather's had a higher heel, which evened things up a bit, since she was five inches shorter than Amy.

"Candy can pick up a pair next week," Natalie said. "Hooray! We're done!"

A few minutes later, the bride waved farewell, since she'd parked near a different exit than her friends. As Heather and Amy sauntered in the opposite direction, Heather said, "Now that we've got a moment alone, I'd like to ask a favor."

"Is it baby-sitting? I don't have much experience, but I'd be glad to give it a try." Amy had been fascinated by the babies she'd seen through the nursery window en route to talk to Quent on Friday.

"Thanks, but it's not baby-sitting," Heather said. "It's about the Moms in Training program."

Both women volunteered at a program for pregnant teenagers. Amy offered counseling and collected donations from the community to help the young women. Heather gave advice about healthy pregnancies. In private conversations with some of the girls, she had also confided about her own experiences as an unwed mother and how adoption had helped her get her life on track.

"What can I do?" Amy asked.

"I'd like a pediatrician to come discuss child development. The director asked me to try to set something up for next Saturday. It's Thanksgiving weekend, but most of the girls want to meet anyway." Heather tore herself away from the shop window. "I'd also like you both to talk a little about child discipline."

"Great idea," Amy said. "I'd be glad to help."

They were passing her favorite video-game store, and she couldn't resist eyeing the display. Half hidden in one corner was a copy of Global Oofstinker, a goofy game about a cartoon skunk trying to take over the world.

The reviews had been mediocre, and so were the sales. Too bad. The manufacturer, WiseWorld Global Productions, had promised a donation to the Doctors Circle's Endowment Fund drive, but the size of the donation was pegged to the game's success.

"The favor I'm asking involves more than just your participation." Heather gave an embarrassed cough.

"Well, don't have a hacking fit on my account," Amy said. "Spit it out."

Heather laughed. "I should have known to get to the point with you."

"Always!"

"I'd like you to ask Quentin Ladd to give the talk," her friend said as they strolled. "Whoever joins us is likely to hear about Olive and Ginger. You know how strongly I feel about my privacy."

"And we both know how the tongues can wag at Doctors Circle," Amy noted.

"Natalie says everyone's been speculating about the reasons for my personal leave. It would be too good a tidbit for one of the older doctors to keep to himself."

"Whereas Quent's new on the block," Amy finished for her. "And he's a great guy. He won't shoot his mouth off if we ask him not to."

"Exactly," Heather said. "So you'll talk to him?"

"You bet."

Amy didn't know why, underneath her confidence, she felt a tremor of uncertainty. She and Quent were buds, right? Why shouldn't she ask him?

She and Heather emerged into crisp sunshine, yesterday's bad weather having vanished with the sea breezes. Amy said goodbye and didn't give the subject of Quentin another thought for at least, oh, thirty seconds.

She wasn't thrilled that Heather had asked her to include him in yet another aspect of her life. They'd have to work closely together on their presentation about discipline.

Talk about discipline! When it came to Quent, Amy needed some of her own. She'd thought of him first thing this morning, kissing her until her lips were swollen. Pulling her onto his lap. Rubbing her breasts.

Still, inviting him to speak was for the good of the young moms-to-be, so she'd do it. Amy got into her car and sat there enjoying the warmth after the briskness of the November day. Heck, she told herself, she could deal with Quent and any feelings that might crop up.

Her dad had always told her that, whenever she found herself in a difficult situation, she should take charge. "Don't wait for other people to come to your rescue," he'd said. "If you want something, go for it."

That advice had helped Amy become a star in high-school sports. Unfortunately, it hadn't worked as well when, tired of being the gawky kid who sat home on Saturday nights, she'd applied it to boys.

After she'd commandeered a couple of dates for school dances during her sophomore year, the guys she liked started to edge away when they saw her coming. At last someone admitted that she'd earned the nickname "The Bulldozer." Embarrassed, Amy had decided to back off and wait until a boy asked her out first.

She'd spent the rest of high school waiting. After a while, she'd been accepted back as one of the guys, but she never seemed to light any romantic fires.

Well, she wasn't going to ask Quent to a dance, Amy reminded herself. It was his professional skills she required, nothing more.

HER FIRST CLIENTS on Monday morning were parents whose three-year-old son had become disruptive after the recent birth of a baby sister. They were happy to receive a list of suggestions, including spending time alone with the preschooler and making sure visitors paid him plenty of attention.

"We think of him as grown-up in comparison to the baby," the mother said. "Now I realize he's still a baby himself."

Amy was glad to help. She wished she had more personal experience with young children to contribute, but thank goodness there were experts to rely on. Plus, she'd always had an instinctive sympathy for kids, a sensitivity to the needs and emotions they weren't able to voice.

When she opened the door at the end of the session, the sharp smell of paint wafted in from the hallway. Her clients said goodbye, then picked their way out through a maze of stepladders and spattered drop cloths.

The whole complex, including the east and west office wings and the three-story Birthing Center, was getting a face-lift. Amy liked the new colors of yellow, aqua and mint green, although she wasn't crazy about the odor that pervaded the west wing, where she worked.

She especially wasn't looking forward to the disruption when her own office got painted. Still, the beige walls could use freshening and she'd decided to have the worn couch and chairs recovered. Also, she was tired of the framed photographs of children and young couples, and this would give her a good excuse to replace them.

The idea of redecorating reminded Amy of her condo, so she put in a call to her association's manager. The news was not good.

The weekend's storm had done considerable damage around town, and most repairmen had more work than they could handle, he told her. Although the tree had been removed and his handyman had nailed boards into place, no roofers would be available for several weeks.

There was some good news, though, he said. The building inspector had left word that she could move back in during the interim.

Sure she could, Amy thought, as long as she didn't mind a mildewing carpet and the messed-up ceiling. She planned to replace them, but that would take time, too.

Until the place was finished, Aunt Mary's house was a better bet for her peace of mind. Although her aunt ran a small day-care center downstairs on weekdays, the large, comfortable home was quiet at other times.

Amy thanked the manager, hung up and fetched a

cup of coffee from the break room. Resolutely, she put the condo out of her mind and turned her attention to two job applicants who'd arrived for their screening tests. As the only full-time psychologist at Doctors Circle, Amy handled a range of tasks involving staff members as well as patient families.

While she waited for the pair to finish the written tests, she tried not to wince at the whine of saws echoing from across the medical complex. The east wing's lower floor was being remodeled into an expanded infertility center, scheduled to open in April. An infertility expert named Jason Carmichael had been hired as the director.

After her two charges departed, Amy met with a new mother and her husband who needed help dealing with the woman's overbearing parents. Talking earnestly, they overstayed their hour, and Amy was too absorbed to cut them off.

By the time they left, she had less than thirty minutes for lunch. From a drawer, she removed a packaged tuna salad kit.

"Eating at your desk isn't healthy, you know." Under cover of the racket from across the way, Quent had arrived in her doorway undetected. He didn't have far to travel, since his clinic was down the hall.

Above the white coat and stethoscope, his blond hair flopped raffishly onto his forehead. Despite her resolve to keep her distance, Amy's spirits leaped.

"Don't tell me you have time to go out for a three-course meal," she said.

"I planned to invite you to take your repast with me in the courtyard." He quirked an eyebrow. "Want to come?"

The office wings flanked a center court. Its tiled fountain, coffee kiosk, benches and round concrete tables made it a popular spot for lunch.

"I can't. I've got an appointment at one." The way Quent was grinning at her, Amy wondered if she'd dabbed mayonnaise on her nose. She stifled the instinct to check a hand mirror, but she couldn't stop herself from patting her French braid to make sure her hair remained in place.

"Why are you wiggling so much? It makes you look twitchy," he said.

"Is that like bewitching?"

"It's more like itchy," Quent joked. "It must be all the noise and smell around here. You should come with me to the Casbah."

"That sounds faintly indecent." Oops. She didn't want to ruin her "been there, done that" image. "Not that I'm against moral decadence, but not on my lunch break."

"Okay. Why don't you come over to my apartment tonight instead?" he said. "I'm working the late shift but I'll be done by seven."

Before Saturday, Amy hadn't worried about giving Quent the wrong idea because he treated her like one of the boys, but that had changed. "What are you proposing?"

"How about Ping-Pong, followed by getting to know each other a little better?" He waggled one eyebrow suggestively, à la Groucho Marx.

"You have a Ping-Pong table in your apartment?" It didn't fit with her mental image of a seductive bachelor pad.

"It was either that or a pool table, and Ping-Pong is more portable in case I have to move," he said. "How about it?"

She'd love to play. But that wasn't all he had in mind, and Amy knew where it would lead. "No, thanks."

Quent regarded her with a crestfallen expression. "Is it my breath?"

"No!" Amy laughed. "It's just…I mean, I'd rather keep it light. I already told you…" An idea hit her. "Actually, there is something I want to discuss."

"Great!" He beamed at her, lighting up the room. "We can talk over pizza at my place."

"We can discuss it now." She checked her watch. Fifteen minutes to go. "It's about the Moms in Training program."

"Something I can help with?" Quent straightened. "I'd be glad to."

Amy explained Heather's request about the presentations. "You're the expert on infant development. When it comes to child discipline, you could provide a pediatrician's perspective and I could discuss it from a counseling perspective."

Quent was all business now. "It would be my pleasure, but shouldn't you pick a doctor who has kids of his own?"

Amy decided to level with him. "There's another matter involved that calls for discretion, and I'm afraid the other doctors might be tempted to gossip. It concerns Heather."

"What about her?"

She searched for a way to explain without revealing too much. "About the reason she took leave. It's likely to come out when you visit the center."

"What's all the mystery?" Quent asked.

"It's not my story to tell," Amy said. "I'd just ask that you keep anything you learn confidential."

"Okay. I promise not to blab any deep dark secrets."

After a moment's thought, Quent added, "You realize we're going to have to meet to prepare our joint program."

Amy was about to say they could do it at the office, when she realized it wouldn't be appropriate. Although her involvement with the young mothers was good public relations for Doctors Circle, it was a volunteer job and shouldn't be done on her work time. "I suppose so."

"Which brings us full circle," Quent said cheerfully. "Seven o'clock at my place. I'll buy the pizza." He wrote the address on a scratch pad and handed it to her. "We'll keep it strictly on the up and up. Unless, by mutual consent, we decide to lie down on the job."

"Don't count on it."

"A guy can hope, can't he?"

A figure appeared behind Quent in the doorway. Gray of complexion, with pouches that gave his eyes a perpetual squint, Dr. Dudley Fingger wore the frown of a disapproving bureaucrat. "There you are, Dr. Ladd. You were due back from lunch five minutes ago."

"Really?" Quent looked at his watch, then made a show of putting it to his ear, frowning and shaking it.

Amy hid a smile. Dr. Fingger was a fussbudget whose plodding sternness never failed to stimulate Quent's penchant for teasing.

Seniority had led to Dudley Fingger's appointment one month ago as temporary director of the Well-Baby Clinic. His predecessor, Dr. Spencer Sorrell, had been a pompous bully whose departure had been cause for celebration.

"The gift shop carries an excellent selection of watches," Dr. Fingger said solemnly.

"I'll check it out. Should I go there now?" Quent asked with pretended earnestness.

"You have patients waiting!"

"Oh, I see," Quent answered. "I guess I should go back to work then, huh?"

"Yes, you should," said his supervisor. "Sorry to disturb you, Ms. Ravenna."

"No problem." Amy wondered if she should suggest that the strait-laced pediatrician address her as "Doctor," just to amuse Quent, but decided against it.

Given his nature, Dr. Fingger would no doubt go around insisting that everyone call her Dr. Ravenna. Although she'd earned her Ph.D., she didn't like to use the title in case people got the mistaken idea that she was a physician.

Quent started off, then returned to poke his head in the door. "Tonight." With a wink, he scooted away.

Amy chuckled. What a scoundrel!

She sobered at the realization that she would be spending the evening alone with Quent. She'd have to rely on her strength of will to keep him at arm's length.

It wasn't going to be easy.

Chapter Four

Amy tried on two outfits while deciding what to wear to Quent's house. If she'd had any more clothes with her, she would have tried those on, too.

"This must be some hot date," said her cousin Kitty, who'd popped in to visit and was reclining atop the brightly colored comforter on the double bed. At seventeen, she had an outgoing nature and plenty of curiosity.

Unfortunately, there was no question of borrowing her clothes. Not only was she shorter than Amy, but she preferred skin-tight pants and tops.

"I'm just going to see my friend Quent." Amy turned sideways to study her jeans and pink turtleneck in the full-length mirror. "We've got some work-related stuff to discuss."

If she wanted to look her best, she was going to have to buy a mirror like this when she got back into her condo, she decided. Or maybe she should give away every mirror she owned and put on her makeup by feel. There was much to be said for giving your appearance as little thought as possible.

"I'll bet he's cute." Kitty flipped back a long strand of brown hair.

"He is," Amy agreed. "But he's not for me."

"Why not?"

"Too much of a playboy," she said.

"If he's in love with you, he'll change," advised her cousin with wisdom accumulated from years of watching TV shows.

"He's not in love with me." Amy shrugged off the pink turtleneck and returned to her first choice, a blue work shirt.

"He never will be, either, if you dress like a boy!" Kitty said. "No offense or anything."

"Don't you have homework to do?"

Her cousin heaved an exaggerated sigh, the kind that teenagers reserve for grown-ups. "I do my homework after dinner."

"Your mom doesn't make you do it first? Lucky you! My dad was really strict," Amy said.

"Mom says parents have to pick their battles. As long as I keep my grades up and help out with the day-care kids during school break, she doesn't nag me."

That bit of motherly wisdom made sense to Amy. She stored it away to share with the Moms in Training.

After tucking in the work shirt, she decided she looked fine for tonight. The only thing she lacked was a coat.

"Do you have a jacket I could borrow?" She made a mental note to stop by her condo and pick up more clothes, now that she was allowed inside.

"Take whatever you want," Kitty said. "It's the least I can do after you loaned me your car last night."

"That was an emergency." An ailing neighbor had needed help picking up her medication. Since Aunt Mary was out, the teenager had volunteered to go.

"I like helping people," Kitty said.

"You've matured a lot." Amy regarded her young cousin affectionately. "You've been a good sport about my moving in like this. I hope I'm not getting in your way."

"It's fun having you here." Kitty sat up on the bed. "When the little kids go home, it gets too quiet. I wish Dad would hurry back."

"I know he misses you a lot, too." Uncle Will, an engineer with a multinational company, was on long-term assignment overseas. It was his third stretch of being gone for months at a time but, Aunt Mary had explained, in another year he'd be able to take early retirement.

Amy hoped that, when she got married, she never had to be separated from her husband for more than a day or so. That was, assuming she ever found the right man.

Of course, women these days didn't have to get married to lead fulfilling lives, she reminded herself. She had an interesting job and plenty of friends. That ought to be enough.

But it wasn't.

Out of nowhere came an image of Quent in a tuxedo, standing in a church with love written on his face as she, Amy Ravenna, sailed toward him in a wedding dress. Not just a church, but a vast cathedral-like expanse of high arches and stained-glass windows; not simply a wedding dress, but a designer extravaganza spun from yards of silk and lace; not merely love, but utter adoration…

What was she thinking? Amy wouldn't have the slightest idea how to plan a wedding like that! And as for Quent, he'd stated soon after they met that he wasn't the marrying kind.

"I gotta go help with dinner." Kitty hopped to her feet. "Good luck tonight."

"I don't need good luck. He's a friend," Amy said, and went to her cousin's room to borrow a jacket.

WHEN HE'D RENTED his apartment, Quent had gotten a kick out of decorating it to suit his own taste and no one else's. Now he wished he'd given more thought to the future.

The large recliner in one corner was about as far from seductive as furniture could get, and while that clunky lamp provided lots of reading light, it wasn't likely to inspire Amy to do a striptease. He didn't even have a couch, just a bunch of plastic chairs clustered around the Ping-Pong table. Well, there was nothing he could do about it now.

Leaving the pizza box and take-out soft drinks next to the net, Quent went into the bathroom to remove his contact lenses. The paint fumes at work made them sting after a while, and it would feel good to put his glasses on.

They didn't look bad, he thought a minute later, regarding the frames in the mirror. In fact, they added a touch of class.

When he was younger, he'd figured most women would find him more attractive with contacts, but he doubted Amy cared. What a relief not to worry about something so superficial, he thought, and went to the kitchen to get paper plates.

THE GLASSES gave Quent a sexy, mature look, Amy thought when he opened the door. The contemporary shape of the rims emphasized the blue of his eyes and the strong contours of his cheekbones.

"I like them," she said after studying him for a moment.

"These?" Absentmindedly, he pushed up the bridge. "They're comfortable, I'll say that."

"You should wear glasses all the time. They're cute." She stepped inside and got her first clear look at the apartment.

Amy nearly laughed in relief. While she'd been imagining a den of iniquity, all she saw were the Ping-Pong table, a recliner, a few resin chairs and, in one corner, a tier of audiovisual equipment.

"The kitchen table is tiny," Quent said. "I figured we could eat out here on the Ping-Pong table, if you don't mind."

"Sounds like fun," she said. "We can pretend we're having afternoon tea at Wimbledon. In miniature, of course."

"Wimbledon. Isn't that a race track?" he asked as he opened the pizza box.

"It's a tennis court in Great Britain."

"Oh, right." From a sack, he extracted napkins. "So you've been to England?"

"A couple of years ago." Amy used most of her vacation weeks for travel.

"Where else have you gone?"

"One year I did a whirlwind tour of Europe," she said. "Another trip, I went to Washington, D.C., and New York City. I love historic sites."

"I knew you were a woman of the world, but I didn't realize the extent of it," Quent teased. "Let's see…I went to Tijuana a few times." The Mexican border town lay a few miles south of San Diego.

"It's a start," Amy said. "Did you enjoy it?"

"Mostly I shopped. The last time, I bought a poncho

and some toys for my niece and nephew,'' he said. ''And practiced my high-school Spanish on the natives. They were very patient.''

''Do you plan to travel more?''

''I guess so.''

They seemed to have run out of things to say. Always before, they'd chattered away about sports, favorite shows on television—they both enjoyed science fiction—or whatever was in the news.

Tonight, Amy felt stiff and self-conscious. She decided it must be due to hunger. Once they started eating, they'd bounce back to normal.

When she pulled up a chair, the Ping-Pong table proved an awkward height, but she supposed there were advantages to having her food closer to her mouth. Less likelihood of spilling it on herself, for instance. ''Oh, good, you got pepperoni.''

''Everybody likes pepperoni.'' Quent distributed slices onto paper plates.

''Not vegetarians,'' she said.

''Everybody except vegetarians.'' When he sat down and stretched his long legs, they brushed hers. A shiver ran through Amy. ''Sorry.''

''Don't worry about it.'' She tried not to think about how much she'd enjoyed that brief contact. Then she remembered the purpose of their meeting, and seized on it gladly. ''I brought a list of topics for us to discuss.'' Amy nodded toward a file folder she'd set next to the pizza box.

Quent swallowed a bite of pizza. ''Just because I'm not bubbling with conversation doesn't mean I need prompting.''

''About child discipline,'' she said.

''Oh, right.'' It was hard to read his expression behind the glasses. "Do you subscribe to any particular theory?"

"Love and communication." To Amy, those were the keys to any relationship.

"How about safety?" Quent said.

"That's important," she agreed. "But I don't see what that has to do with discipline."

"What if love and communication don't stop a child from trying to knock over the baby's crib?"

"I'll have to think about that one," Amy admitted.

Quent downed what must be his third or fourth slice. "Want more?"

"No, thanks." She'd had three pieces, which was her limit.

"Great!" He gave an apologetic shake of the head. "That didn't come out right. I meant, if you're sure you've had enough, I'll save the rest for breakfast."

"I used to love pizza for breakfast when I was a teenager," Amy said.

"Wow." Quent stood and closed the box. "I've never met a woman who understood about eating pizza for breakfast. Most of them think it's gross."

"It comes from growing up in a house full of guys," she said. "Ready for Ping-Pong?"

"You bet," he said.

"We can go over ideas for the presentations while we play." Amy, like Quent, was kinesthetic, which meant she learned and thought best while in motion.

After he put the pizza away, they tossed the paper plates in a wastebasket. Soon they were slamming the ball back and forth almost as fast as they volleyed remarks about how to discipline children.

The problem was that they didn't see eye-to-eye. Amy believed explanations and careful listening were

vital to teaching children the rules. Quent stressed time-
outs and suspension of privileges for disobedience.

He served the ball without losing the flow of their
conversation. "Personally, I think there are kids who
benefit from the occasional mild spanking. Since these
young mothers may not understand the difference between appropriate punishment and hitting a child in an-
ger, though, I'll leave that out."

"You believe in spanking?" Amy was so shocked,
she barely managed to return his shot. "I would never
spank a child!"

"What if he kept running into traffic?" Quent
slammed a ball right by her. "My point."

"I thought we weren't keeping score." They'd
agreed that conducting a formal game would interfere
with their work.

"Doesn't matter. I still like knowing I won the
point." He grinned.

"It depends which point we're talking about. I don't
agree about spanking," Amy said as she retrieved the
ball from behind a stereo speaker. "My dad never
spanked us, and we didn't run into traffic."

"Maybe he didn't spank you because you weren't the
kind of kids who needed to be spanked."

"You're baiting me."

"You just hate to admit I'm right."

She glared. Quent laughed. "Don't worry. I promise
not to mention corporal punishment in our talk."

"Good." After a moment's consideration, she said,
"I think it's okay for us to have differing opinions as
long as we agree on the main issues."

"Sounds good to me," he said. "When are we giving
these talks?"

"Saturday morning, if you're free." Amy had forgotten to mention the short notice. "I know it's the Thanksgiving holiday, but most of the girls will be there."

"No problem. I'm on duty, so I'll be around," Quent said. "The department has some charts I can use."

"Great!"

Amy was glad to get the matter settled. Quent looked so appealing with his blond hair ruffled and his polo shirt clinging to his chest that she had a hard time thinking about the presentation.

If there'd been a couch, she would have been tempted to push him onto it. But the very thought of trying to curl against him in the awkwardness of a recliner suggested a humorous rather than amorous result.

"So how many kids do you want to have?" Quent asked.

Surprised by the question, Amy lost her concentration and served the ball into the net. "Why do you assume I want kids?"

"When you were staring at those babies at the birthing center, you had a look on your face like…like…"

"Like what?"

"Like you wanted to hold one in your arms."

"Sure. They're cute. Big deal." The last thing she wanted was for him or anyone to feel sorry for her. So what if she hadn't been able to make her dreams come true? There was plenty of time left.

Yet for some reason, she served the ball so hard it nearly missed the table. It chipped off the edge at an angle and shot by him.

"Foul!" Quent called as he went after the ball.

"It is not!" She refused to concede, even though she suspected he was right. Besides, they weren't supposed to be playing for real.

"It was over the line."

"There is no line." The table, which he must have bought secondhand, had faded. Amy saw nothing wrong with using that fact to her advantage.

"Everybody knows there's a line." Quent returned to his place. "However, I'll concede if you answer my question."

"Which question?"

"How many children do you want?"

"I never thought beyond one," she said.

One child to hold in her arms. One cradle to rock. One tiny pair of upraised arms and one little face gazing at her lovingly. It seemed like a whole universe.

To Amy's annoyance, his serve whizzed past her. The man had an annoying way of distracting her.

"One?" Quent shook his head, which made his glasses slip lower. "I picture you as an earth mother. Three or four at least."

"Then I'd better start soon. Not tonight, however," she added in case he misinterpreted her remark.

Quent reddened. "I wasn't implying that you should. I hadn't even thought that far."

It was time to quit dancing around the obvious. "Don't tell me you haven't had sex on your mind since we nearly got beaned by that palm tree," Amy said. "Well, get over it."

"How about you?" he demanded. "You've been thinking about it, too, or you wouldn't have mentioned it."

Too late, she saw the trap she'd set for herself by raising the issue. It would be unthinkable to tell the truth about her lack of experience and how much making love would mean to her. Instead, she said, "You're my buddy. We'd both regret it if we yielded to impulse."

"I'm not so sure," Quent said. "Maybe we ought to go ahead and get it out of our systems."

His words stung. Was it possible that making love, which would turn her life upside down, would cure Quent of any feelings for her whatsoever?

Although he didn't seem like the cruel type, Amy knew that men sometimes behaved coldheartedly toward the women they'd "conquered." The prospect was too painful to contemplate.

Struggling to keep her tone light, she said, "I don't know when I've received such a romantic offer. Who needs flowers, wine and trips to Tahiti when a man whispers in your ear—what was that again?—'Let's get it out of our systems.'"

Quent had the grace to look ashamed of himself. "I'm sorry. That was rude."

"Apology accepted."

"I don't mean to be pushy," he went on, "but it's hard on a guy, knowing how great you must be, imagining all the things you can teach me."

What on earth was he talking about? Amy supposed she should order an advanced sex manual on the Internet and find out. Even if she did, however, she still wouldn't know how to put it into practice.

If only she dared level with him. But she'd grown up with guys and knew how he would react. Men didn't sympathize about stuff like being a virgin. Quent would tease her mercilessly, and Amy, for all her apparent self-confidence, was sensitive on the subject.

"I guess you'll just have to suffer," she said.

"It's your choice," Quent told her. "You're the one who brought up sex. I won't pretend I'm not very attracted to you, Amy, but I didn't mean to make you uncomfortable."

"It's natural to fantasize," she conceded, "but you ought to picture someone other than me." Perhaps a movie star, she thought.

"Any suggestions?" He smiled. "I'll settle for names and phone numbers."

Amy hadn't meant a person who might actually take him to bed. It bothered her that Quent was so willing to transfer his interest. "I'm sure you've got a little black book already." She grabbed her purse and stuffed her notes into the file folder. This conversation had become too painful to continue. "I have to run."

"What's the hurry?" A pucker formed between his eyebrows. "Got a late date?"

"Sure. I stack 'em up every night. Two, three in a row." How could he be so blind? Amy wondered.

"Sorry, I shouldn't have made that assumption." Obviously, he'd caught the irony in her tone. "You hadn't mentioned anyone in particular but I figured you must be seeing somebody."

"Even Cleopatra had dry spells," Amy said, and hurried out.

HE'D BLOWN IT, Quent mused as he flopped onto the bed. For once, he ignored the remote control and lay there staring at the ceiling.

Only an idiot propositioned a woman by suggesting they "get it out of our systems." She'd been right about his being romantically challenged.

Did men really court her with flowers, wine and trips to Tahiti? Probably, Quent thought. It was easy to contemplate whisking her away to a South Seas island for a weekend of lovemaking.

If he wanted to get closer to Amy, it was time he started taking a suave approach, the kind that involved sending bouquets and dancing in each other's arms instead of playing Ping-Pong. He wished he could afford to buy her some jewelry, perhaps a gemstone to match her eyes.

Except, Quent realized, he didn't know what color Amy's eyes were. Dark brown or black? He doubted a gem in either of those colors would look terribly romantic.

He had a lot to learn about the sophisticated approach. Maybe he could glean some hints by watching old movies on TV, the kind that starred Cary Grant or Fred Astaire.

Eager to begin his research, he reached for the newspaper and skimmed the listings, searching for something appropriate. Wait! There was a Jackie Chan movie starting in five minutes.

Okay, he'd watch that first, and then find a woman-type movie later, even if he had to stay awake till dawn. Once he decided on a course of action, Quent didn't give up easily.

Chapter Five

She and her aunt prepared turkey and their favorite side dishes. "I'm sorry your friend Quent couldn't join us," Mary said as she carved the turkey at the head of the table.

"He had to work." Amy set out a baking dish of sweet potatoes. Several of her aunt's and cousin's friends would be arriving soon. "Babies don't pick convenient hours to be born, unfortunately."

"Kitty was born at 3:00 a.m. I'd been awake so long, I fell asleep with her in my arms," her aunt admitted.

Tall and solidly built, she had a down-to-earth, cheerful air. After Amy's mother decamped, her only female role model had been her aunt. Although they didn't live near each other, they'd often talked by phone, and Mary had helped her through some difficult times.

"I'd like to meet Quent one of these days," her aunt said. "I've never seen your face light up the way it does when you mention him."

"I'm afraid he doesn't feel the same way," Amy admitted. "He has the usual male urges that any man gets around a woman, I suppose, but he thinks of me as his pal, not his girlfriend."

"What's he look like?"

"Blond hair, blue eyes. The nurses and receptionists sigh about him as if he were a movie star," she said.

"He must be drawn to you whether he knows it or not, or he wouldn't spend so much time hanging around." Her aunt set aside some scraps for the neighborhood cats. "If he's as sharp as you indicate, he'll wake up and smell the coffee one of these days."

"One of these centuries, maybe." From the kitchen, Amy heard the timer ding. "Sounds like the apple pie's done."

"Where's Kitty? She's supposed to be helping."

"Still in the bathroom." Amy chuckled. "Oh, let teenagers be teenagers, Aunt Mary."

The older woman considered briefly. "She can be on cleanup detail."

Soon afterwards, Kitty came downstairs and the guests began ringing the doorbell. The group of them had a merry time. Conversation flowed and everyone ate seconds, although they made only a dent in the bounty.

Afterwards, seeing the piles of food that remained, Amy decided to take a plate to Quent at the Birthing Center. She found him sitting in the doctors' lounge eating a candy bar and reading a medical journal.

"I hope that's not all you had to eat today," she said.

Quent sniffed the air appreciatively. "If I say yes, will you bring me seconds?"

"Don't get greedy." Grateful for her aunt's multi-level pie carrier, Amy produced two paper plates full of food plus two slabs of pie, one apple and one pumpkin.

"You cooked all this with those shapely hands of yours?" Quent took the flatware with an air of reverence. "It's beyond perfect."

"Aunt Mary did most of it." Amy sat on an adjacent

couch. There was no one else in the lounge, only the shiny hardness of snack machines for company. "Have you been busy today?"

"One breech birth and one preemie." Although as a pediatrician Quent could examine any newborn, his special skills made him most in demand for difficult births. "They're both doing well."

While he ate, Amy described the friends and relatives who'd attended the dinner and the welcome phone call that had come from her uncle. Not until Quent was halfway through dessert did she ask, "What time are you off?"

"In half an hour unless they need me." He reached for his second slice of pie. "Did you have something in mind?"

Through the lingering traces of antiseptic, Amy could smell Quent's heated masculinity. All it took was one whiff and her body responded with an unfamiliar urgency. She definitely had something in mind, but she didn't care to mention it.

"Maybe a video game or something," she said. "Unless you're too tired."

"I always have enough energy for a few rounds of video games." Quent tapped his fingers on his knee, as if a new thought had just occurred to him. "Or how about a moonlit drive instead? We could watch the stars shine over the ocean and listen to the waves splash against the shore."

Amy waited for the punch line. It didn't come. "Now I know you're way past exhausted," she said.

"What makes you say that?"

"You're getting spacey."

"Maybe I'm getting romantic."

He couldn't be serious. "If pie does this to you, I'll

keep that in mind for Valentine's Day.'' She began clearing the dirty paper plates and collecting the flatware. ''Maybe it'll inspire you to spring for a box of chocolates.''

''It isn't the pie...'' Quent's beeper went off. To Amy, it was almost a relief when, after checking it, he announced wryly that he'd been summoned.

Whatever joke he'd been playing, its similarity to her dreams was much too painful. ''Have a good time,'' she told him, and made her getaway.

ALTHOUGH FRIDAY was a holiday for most people, Amy had scheduled patients because of her heavy caseload. In her office, the smell of paint remained strong, forcing her to keep the window open. The workmen had painted it on Wednesday and she'd hoped it would be back to normal by now, but no such luck.

Disruption must be in the stars, Amy thought, since she'd been affected both at home and at work. She wondered if the heavens had any more surprises in store for her, and hoped they'd be good ones.

Still, she liked the freshness of her walls, which had been painted pale green with two-toned trim. She hoped she could find suitable pictures.

Her last patient of the day was Loretta Arista, the public relations director for Doctors Circle. It was her third session, and this time she didn't bring her husband.

''It's my problem, not Mario's. I'm the one obsessing about not being able to have a baby,'' explained Loretta, who looked brisk and businesslike in a tailored suit. The woman, who wore a dramatic white streak in her dark hair, spoke in a forceful manner.

Now thirty-four, Loretta had been trying to get pregnant since her late twenties. She'd been under even more internal pressure since learning that her sister, Rita, six years her junior, was expecting triplets in May.

Although Loretta and her husband had gone through the home-study process, legally required before adoption, they'd hesitated about seeking a baby because they'd heard how difficult it was. Or, at least, that was the reason the P.R. director had given in the past.

Now she leaned forward, her elbows on her knees. "I come from a tight-knit Hispanic family. All my cousins have kids, and now my sister's expecting triplets. I'm afraid adopted children wouldn't fit in."

"How would you feel about bringing adopted children to a family gathering?" To Amy, Loretta's emotions, not the reactions of her relatives, were the real issue.

"I'd feel like a failure," her client admitted.

"Aha," said Amy.

"Yes. Aha." Loretta shook her head. "I can't get past the sense that this is my fault. I ought to be able to overcome infertility if I struggle hard enough."

"You're accustomed to taking control of your life."

"You bet I am," Loretta said. "Only this time I can't."

"And that's hard to face."

"Very hard." The other woman fell silent for a moment before continuing, "Well, Dr. Carmichael will be here in a few months and I want to give him a try. If he can't make it happen, maybe it's not meant to be."

It was the first time Loretta had mentioned the possibility of remaining childless. She grew more cheerful as she and Amy discussed it, perhaps because at least she had a choice about her future.

When the session ended, the two of them strolled down the hall together. The drop cloths and ladders were gone, the workmen having moved to another part of the building, but the place still reeked.

They stopped at the department secretary's desk. Nan Ryerson, a widow in her sixties, had been on the job only two weeks, hired after her predecessor left to join the Peace Corps. Her good nature and mature competence were proving to be assets.

"Hi, there," Nan greeted Loretta. "I'll be right with you."

She turned back to a young woman with collar-length dark hair. Amy recognized her as a nurse, Cynthia Hernandez, who worked on the second floor. Usually, Cynthia assisted Heather, but during her leave was helping another doctor.

The young woman clenched her jaw so tightly that Amy could almost hear her teeth grinding. Nan handed her an appointment card. "We'll see you next week."

"Fine." The nurse hurried away without meeting anyone's eyes.

Whatever was wrong, Amy wished Cynthia didn't have to wait so long for counseling. However, it was five o'clock on a Friday afternoon, too late to see her this week.

One of the most difficult lessons Amy had had to learn was not to take clients' problems personally. Much as she cared about them, she couldn't take responsibility for every setback in their lives.

"I don't think I need another appointment right now," Loretta said. "Let's wait until after Dr. Carmichael arrives and see what happens."

"I'm here if you need me," Amy said. "Have a great weekend."

"You, too."

As soon as Loretta left, Nan, who never seemed in a

hurry to go home, addressed Amy. "I keep hearing about this Dr. Carmichael. You know, I originally applied to be his secretary, but from what I hear, I'm glad I didn't get that job. Plus I like working for you."

"Thanks." Amy chewed over what her secretary had said. "Exactly what have you heard about Dr. Carmichael?"

"That he has a reputation for being high-handed and short-tempered," Nan said. "And that he's great at getting women pregnant."

Amy laughed. "You make him sound like a stud!"

"That's not what I meant. But you can never have too many good-looking guys around." Despite Nan's gray bun and oversize figure, her keen eyes made it clear she defied any stereotypes about old ladies.

"Bringing him to Doctors Circle is a real feather in our cap," Amy told her. "He's very highly regarded. I only met him briefly when he held a press conference here a few months ago, so I can't give you any firsthand impressions."

"If you don't mind my mentioning it, I heard that Dr. Rourke asked for leave right after she learned he was heading the new department. People are wondering if there's some connection," Nan said. "Not that I want to spread rumors. In fact, I'd rather squash them."

"You can definitely squash this one." Amy suspected her secretary meant *quash* rather than *squash*, but she liked the imagery the word presented. "Believe me, Heather's reasons for taking leave had nothing to do with Dr. Carmichael."

She declined to mention that, at the reception following the press conference, Heather had pointedly avoided Jason. Apparently the two had met previously and taken a dislike to each other.

They were both professionals, and she was sure they'd get along as colleagues. Since Heather hadn't mentioned Dr. Carmichael since she'd gone on leave, Amy assumed that whatever had happened wasn't significant.

"I'm glad," Nan said. "I'll spread the word."

"Thanks." That should make things easier for Heather when she returned from leave next week. By the time Jason arrived on staff, the supposed rift between them might be forgotten altogether.

All the same, Amy made a mental note to watch what she said around her new secretary. Although Nan had a good heart, she clearly enjoyed being part of the office grapevine.

Amy locked up her office and went out. Quent had mentioned earlier that he was working tonight. A couple of women with high-risk pregnancies had gone into labor.

Well, there was always someone to hang out with at Aunt Mary's. She had a wide circle of friends, and tonight's schedule included a potluck supper followed by a video double feature. Amy was almost sorry the roofers were due to fix her condo next week.

On her way out, she glanced into the nearly empty waiting room of the Well-Baby Clinic. Her heart leaped when she saw Quent's lean body angled against the front counter. For a moment she contemplated going inside to talk to him.

But he wasn't alone. The pretty young receptionist, Hallie, glowed at him, hanging on every word, and Quent appeared to be lapping it up. Usually he made a joke out of flirting, but now he gazed at the woman intently.

A knot formed in Amy's chest and she tore herself

away. Obviously, there was no shortage of eager candidates for his attention.

Oh, heavens, was she jealous? Amy hated that kind of possessiveness. Nobody was going to put a collar and leash on her, and she had no intention of putting one on Quent, either.

A few steps later, she was startled to find him at her side. "What's your hurry?" he asked. "Your legs are moving so fast, you look like Road Runner."

"I always thought of myself as more the Woody Woodpecker type," she said.

Quent chuckled. "Sorry, I misspoke. I meant to say that suit really brings out the shade of your eyes."

She glanced down to remind herself of what she was wearing. "It's blue."

"I can see that," Quent said.

"My eyes are brown."

"They are?" He blinked a couple of times. "It must be these contacts. They're fogging over."

"Very funny," Amy said.

From behind her, Hallie called, "Dr. Ladd? You're needed in the delivery room."

"Thanks." To Amy, Quent said, "Gotta go."

"I understand."

"By the way," he said, "I knew your eyes were brown."

"Then why…?"

"It was your suit that confused me." He edged away. "The color. It's such a brownish shade of blue."

"Actually, it's navy."

"Okay, so colors aren't my strong point. See you tomorrow." He waved and beat a hasty retreat.

Now what, Amy wondered, had that been about?

CARY GRANT wouldn't have made a mistake like that, but Cary Grant had had scriptwriters. Even so, it was impossible to imagine him botching a simple compliment.

Quent's attempt to be suave had worked great on the receptionist, but he'd bombed the minute he tried it on Amy. He'd have to try again.

Tomorrow morning, after they addressed the Moms in Training, it would be natural for them to go to lunch together. Quent intended to take Amy to a special restaurant.

They could dine at leisure, and he promised himself not to crack stupid jokes. If he acted differently, Amy would see him in a new light. Although he wasn't sure where this was leading, Quent knew he wanted to be more than her buddy.

His strides slowed as he entered the three-story Birthing Center. The main action, as far as Quent was concerned, took place on the first floor, home to the labor and delivery area. The same floor housed antepartum testing, admitting, the gift shop, the cafeteria, the in-patient pharmacy and radiology.

After delivery, patients were transferred to rooms upstairs and babies went to the regular or the intermediate-care nursery on the same floor. Those requiring neonatal intensive care were airlifted to larger hospitals in Long Beach or the city of Orange.

Quent rarely went to the basement level unless there was a meeting in the auditorium. The rest of that floor was devoted to non-obstetrical surgical facilities.

The nurses in labor and delivery were waiting for him. "You need to scrub up right away," the charge nurse told him. "The patient is prepped for her C-section."

"I'm on my way," he said, and put everything out of his mind except the well-being of a tiny patient who was about to enter the world.

THE MOMS IN TRAINING met at the Serene Beach Community Center in Outlook Park. The one-story building presented a comfortable spot for the teenage girls, many of whom had taken summer classes or played basketball there.

At the moment, there were nine girls in the group, ranging in age from fourteen to nineteen. With the encouragement of the volunteer staff and the community center's director, all were continuing their educations.

In a many-windowed classroom, Amy introduced Quent, then moved aside. He gave the girls a smile, and their attention sharpened as they drank him in.

"Hi," he said. "We're going to talk about those little people inside you and how they're growing and changing every day. We'll also discuss what happens to them during the first year after they poke their noses into the world."

A couple of girls giggled. Amy could see that he'd won their interest.

They were a diverse bunch from varied backgrounds. Some slouched in their chairs, others sat straight. Although jeans and maternity tops predominated, one young lady wore an old-fashioned flowered dress, while another let her oversized belly peep out beneath a short top.

After distributing pamphlets on prenatal development, Quent erected a chart showing the unborn baby at landmark stages. Step by step, he took them through the miraculous processes of conception and growth.

"Your child's first environment is the one you create

inside yourself,'' Quent told the rapt group. ''If you wouldn't feed your baby beer, don't drink it yourself. Just imagine a mother who gave her small child nothing but hot dogs and French fries to eat! That's why you need to drink milk and eat lots of fruits and vegetables, because that's what you're feeding junior.''

He went on to discuss the effects of childbirth on the baby and outline the changes that take place during infancy. ''We do have yardsticks that warn us if development is lagging, but don't compare your child to anyone else's. Some perfectly normal kids walk and talk late. Maybe they're stubborn, or perhaps they're deep thinkers.''

When he finished, hands shot up. Patiently, Quent took each question, always showing respect for his audience.

This knowledgeable, steady man was quite a change from the playful friend who boasted when he scored a point at Ping-Pong. There was a tenderness about him that made Amy want to get closer to him. He would make a wonderful father someday, when he was ready for a family. And when he found the right woman.

If only he wanted to settle down now. If only he saw her as a woman to love. If only he weren't guaranteed to break her heart without half trying.

One of the girls kept waving her hand. When Quent called on her, she said, ''What's a neonatologist, anyway?''

''Good question.'' He sat on the edge of a sturdy table. ''A neonatologist is a pediatrician who gets an extra three years' training in treating babies during their earliest months.''

''So, like, how long did you have to go to school?'' asked another girl. ''How old are you?''

"I'm twenty-nine," he said, "which, if you'll forgive me for bragging, is young to complete your training in this field. I graduated from high school when I was sixteen."

"Wow," said another young mother-to-be. "I wish I could do that. How old were you when you finished college?"

"Barely nineteen," Quent said. "Then I went to medical school for four years, followed by an internship, a three-year residency in pediatrics and a residency in neonatology. In case anyone's counting, I'll be thirty in January."

Amy was impressed. She'd earned her master's degree in psychology at twenty-three and her Ph.D. four years later, while working part-time. Quent was way ahead of her.

When he finished, Amy joined him for a discussion of child discipline. They both made the point that consistency and patience were vital, and their audience listened intently.

Afterwards, the girls clustered around Quent, asking questions and, in a couple of cases, flirting. He responded with professional concern and a sense of humor.

"You both did a wonderful job," Heather told them once the mothers-to-be departed. The obstetrician had observed the talk from the back of the room. The program director was out of town this week due to the holiday, so Heather had volunteered to supervise.

"Thanks for inviting me, both of you," Quent answered.

"Our pleasure," she said.

From the intent way Quent was regarding her, Amy got the impression he wanted to talk to her alone. Before she could find a polite way to take him aside, however, Heather's daughter Olive marched into the room holding her two-month-old baby.

"Hey, Mom," she said, "that new Julia Roberts movie starts in half an hour. I think Ginger's tired enough to sleep through it. You want to come with us?"

"Sure." Only a blink gave away Heather's momentary discomfort at having her secret revealed.

If Olive hadn't called her "Mom," the relationship might have escaped detection. The daughter was taller and had dark hair, although baby Ginger's red fuzz echoed her grandmother's shade.

"Is this your granddaughter?" Clearly, Quent had made the connection. "Congratulations!"

"Thanks." Heather made introductions as smoothly as if she hadn't been knocking herself out for months to keep her family out of view. When pleasantries had been exchanged, she said, "I guess we'd better go get our tickets before the theater sells out."

"My thought exactly," Olive said. "Anyone else want to come?"

"No, thanks," Amy said.

"I'll pass," Quent added.

They were left alone in the classroom. "I don't need to ask you not to mention Olive and Ginger at work, right?" Amy went on to explain how Heather had given her daughter up for adoption and then found her again.

"She has no reason to be ashamed of them," Quent pointed out.

"She isn't. Far from it," Amy said. "Heather values her privacy. It must have been very painful for her, first being abandoned by the man she loved, then relinquishing her child. She doesn't want the gossips chewing over every detail."

"I won't say a word." From the way Quent's jaw worked, Amy gathered he was concentrating his thoughts, so she kept quiet and waited.

He seemed more reserved than usual. Had something happened that she didn't know about?

Their friendship had grown quickly and spontaneously. In a few short months, he'd come to mean a great deal to her, and yet, she realized, there was much she didn't know about him.

"We could go out for lunch." He gave an impatient frown, apparently directed at himself. "That's not how I meant to say it. Amy, would you care to have lunch with me?"

"Why not?" Judging by his expression, her response fell short of his hopes. "What's going on?"

"What do you mean?"

"You seem different today," she said.

"That's good." Daylight from the windows played across Quent's tanned face. "Not that I expect to measure up to your usual standards, but…" In his pocket, the phone rang.

"Are you on call?" Amy asked.

"No." Frowning, he answered it. "Dr. Ladd here. Hi, Lucy…. How bad is it?…That doesn't sound too… Yes, I understand. Of course, I'll come right away. Don't worry. See you in a while." He rang off.

Amy itched to ask who had been on the line, but it was none of her business. Maybe a relative, she thought. Quent never talked much about his family, although he'd mentioned his father and a niece and nephew.

"I'm sorry. I'll have to take a rain check," he said. "I've got to drive to San Diego. Personal business."

"No problem."

"You're a good sport," he said.

"What are friends for?" She wanted to be so much more, Amy thought. But this wasn't the time to bring it up.

Quent moved closer, as if drawn to her. She reached out and ruffled his hair. It was so soft, she wanted to pull him against her and touch him everywhere.

Quickly, she said, "It was a little flat in one place. I figured I'd fluff it up for you."

"Thanks. I'd hate to go around with flat hair," Quent teased, then sobered. "I'm sorry we'll have to postpone our lunch."

"That's okay." It wasn't as if they hadn't shared hamburgers plenty of times.

After he left, Amy decided to go to the Julia Roberts movie after all. With luck, the on-screen romance would keep her from tormenting herself, at least for a few hours, with the burning question of the day: Who on earth was Lucy?

Chapter Six

Greg held out his hand, palm up, showing a reddened patch on the heel. "It hurts, Uncle Quent."

"I'll bet it does." Sitting beside his nephew on the sofa in the living room of Lucy's apartment, Quent turned the little hand to catch the light. "The damage looks superficial, but I'll bet it smarts like the dickens, doesn't it, little guy?"

Greg nodded solemnly.

"I guess I overreacted." Lucy pushed back a wedge of shaggy, dark-blond hair as she paced through her overstuffed apartment. Toys cluttered the floor, fitting right in with the welter of magazines strewn across the coffee table. "I washed it and applied an antibiotic, but he kept complaining that it hurt."

Earlier, she'd explained that an elderly, hard-of-hearing neighbor had been watching the children while Lucy jogged. Apparently the woman had become so absorbed in keeping up with Tara's toddler antics that she hadn't noticed when Greg went into the kitchen and made popcorn in the microwave. He'd burned his hand on the steam when he opened the bag.

Although only four, Greg considered himself the man of the household and liked to do things for himself. It was time he had a real man around, Quent thought, but as far as he knew, Lucy wasn't seriously involved with anyone.

"It pays to be careful," he told her. "I don't mind your calling me."

"I contacted the pediatrician. He said that if it was serious, I should take Greg to the emergency room." Nervousness made her chatter more than usual. "Who wants to take kids to a place full of sick people at this time of year? They'd catch a cold or worse. I've already used up all my sick leave this year staying home with them."

Quent could see how frazzled she was. He suspected she hadn't been completely ready to become a mother, and maybe she still wasn't.

"You did fine," he said. "Frankly, you've taken on a lot and I wish I could help more."

"Thanks." She stopped pacing. "Are you sure he doesn't need a bandage?"

"Just keep the wound clean and apply more antibiotic in about four hours," Quent said. "Do you have the kind that provides pain relief?"

"I don't think so." Lucy checked the tube she'd left on the arm of the couch. "Nope. I'll ask Jenny in apartment B to run to the drugstore for me. She's only thirteen and she's eager to earn some money."

"I'll pick it up myself. No reason for you to pay anyone. And now that I'm working, I'm going to start sending you a monthly expense check," Quent said, although he knew the grandparents were already chipping in. "I want to do more for the kids."

"Great. I'd like to send Greg to preschool, for one thing," she said.

"He isn't in preschool yet? Don't they offer something like that at your day care?'' Quent had assumed the boy was learning his numbers and colors in preparation for kindergarten.

"No, it's playtime all day," Lucy said. "Don't worry. He's fine."

Quent knew he had no right to criticize, so he backed off. "I'm glad you intend to put him in preschool." He turned to Greg. "I'm going to get some medicine that'll take the hurt away, okay?"

"I knew you'd fix it." The boy gazed up at him with such trust that Quent wanted to do a whole lot more for him. The only thing he could do at the moment was reach out and hug his nephew, so he did.

Tara, who'd been standing by his knee drinking in every word, stuck out her hand. "Ow."

There was no sign of injury, Quent found when he examined it. The hurt, he suspected, lay inside, in the space that should have been filled by her parents' love. Besides, a fifteen-month-old, like a four-year-old, was entitled to lots of affection.

"I guess you need a hug, too." He swept her against him, and caught a whiff of cherry-scented shampoo. What a sweet little girl, he thought, and wondered how he could have stayed away so long.

A year ago, devastated by the loss of his mother, brother and sister-in-law, Quent had scarcely been able to think about the children. When Lucy had offered to take them, he and the other family members had accepted without question.

Now he wondered whether this was a good idea for the long term, despite their aunt's earnest efforts. Not only for the children, but for Lucy, who deserved a life of her own.

Quent released his niece. "Is that better?"

"Yes!" She gave him a heartwarming grin.

After getting directions to the pharmacy, he said, "I'll take you all out to eat when I get back."

"Fried chicken?" Greg asked.

"Absolutely."

"Fwench fwies!" said Tara.

"We'll get those, too," Greg assured her. Although nutrition was important, so was having fun together.

A surge of protectiveness made it hard for him to leave, even for a short time. As he drove to the store, Quent remembered Amy's comment about Heather having been abandoned by the man she loved. How could anyone behave that way? Taking care of the people you loved, the people who trusted you, was essential to being human.

Of course, that didn't mean that you instinctively knew how to handle every situation. Look at the disagreement between him and Amy about discipline.

She'd bristled at the idea of spanking, and Quent had to admit he couldn't see himself ever taking a hand to Greg or Tara. However, having treated children for avoidable injuries, he knew that if parents didn't follow through on their discipline, kids could suffer consequences a lot more serious than a spanking.

He supposed he had a lot to learn about children. So did Amy. No, he meant Lucy, of course. Lucy was the one taking care of his niece and nephew. Amy was simply on his mind because they spent so much time together.

Man, his brain was getting scrambled, Quent reflected as he emerged from his car in the drugstore parking lot. He'd better concentrate on buying the right ointment or he was likely to return with a treatment for hemorrhoids by mistake. And how on earth would he explain that?

THE REST of the day did not go well for Amy.

By the time she arrived at the movie theater, the next showing was sold out, so she went jogging instead. Without Quent, the zing was missing. Worse, she tripped over a curb and scraped her leg.

For dinner, she stopped by a hamburger drive-through.

When she arrived home, Aunt Mary and Kitty invited her to attend a high-school football game, but Amy couldn't summon any enthusiasm.

So she was home alone on a Saturday night, with nothing on TV. Around eight-thirty, she drove to the Paris Bar.

Located in a row of shops in a funky seaside area, the bar made a halfhearted attempt to live up to its name. A faded mural of the Eiffel Tower covered one wall, and a framed poster from *Moulin Rouge* hung above a couple of video-game machines where several men vied intently.

On TV, the Lakers were playing, to the rapt attention of customers who sat imbibing drinks and nibbling corn chips. Amy found a stool at the bar and ordered a beer.

"Is it raining yet?" asked Brian, the bartender. A former athlete sinking into middle-aged pudginess, he liked to chat with his regular customers.

"No. Is it supposed to?" Amy asked. She'd been enjoying the pleasant weather since the last storm.

"You musta missed the forecast," he said.

She groaned. "Great."

"Oh, yeah, I forgot about your roof," Brian said. "Guess you won't be getting that fixed soon."

"That depends on how long the rain lasts."

Brian went to wait on some new arrivals, leaving

Amy to contemplate the question of Lucy's identity. She decided to tackle the subject logically.

Quent had mentioned San Diego, his hometown. It had sounded as if someone were ill, perhaps a member of the family. But if it were a sister or aunt, wouldn't he have explained that?

Lucy might be a former girlfriend, Amy thought with a twist of anxiety. Quent had only moved to Serene Beach a few months ago. He might still be in contact with her.

If he was concerned enough to drive down to San Diego without delay, she must be special. Amy had never considered that he might still harbor feelings for someone else.

She dragged her thoughts away. There was no point in tormenting herself with what-ifs and might-bes.

On TV, the basketball game reached its climactic moments. Among the Lakers' opponents, one player after another lost the ball. Finally a grim-faced athlete, in a desperate last effort, leaped into the air and shot the ball halfway across the court toward the basket. It missed. Dismayed, the man landed off-balance and fell on his butt as the final buzzer sounded.

Most onlookers in the bar shouted their approval, while a couple of their companions muttered unhappily. Folded bills changed hands.

At least Amy wasn't the only person having a bad day, she thought. Misery really did love company.

A hint of moisture blew in as the door opened. She caught a whiff of familiar aftershave lotion and her spirits leaped.

In the mirror behind the bar, she watched Quent approach. His eyes were bright, his movements energetic beneath the English-style raincoat. Apparently he'd had a good time today.

She wasn't going to think about it. Wasn't going to wonder what he and Lucy had been doing. Wasn't going to give it a moment's thought.

"So how'd it go in San Diego?" she blurted in spite of herself as he took the stool beside her.

"Fantastic!" he said. "We were having such a good time, I stayed longer than I meant to."

Surely he wouldn't be so blatant if "having a good time" had included sex, so Amy ventured, "Doing what, exactly?"

"Building a castle," he said. "Hey, Brian, how about a beer?"

"Coming right up."

"You went to the beach in this weather?" Amy asked. "Your friend Lucy must have the hide of a walrus." It always got cold by the ocean this time of year, and, in her experience, constructing a sand castle involved slogging through plenty of wet sand.

"What?" Puzzlement lines formed around his eyes. "I don't follow you."

"You said you and Lucy built a castle," she said.

"Not Lucy and I. Tara and I."

How many girls did he know in San Diego? "Sorry. I thought you said Lucy." Here she'd been obsessing all day over the wrong name! Amy was glad she wasn't the sort of person who stuck pins in voodoo dolls, because she might have harmed an innocent bystander.

"And Greg," Quent said. When his beer arrived, he took a long swallow.

What a relief! "There was a whole group of you?"

"Just Lucy, Tara and Greg. Plus me, of course." He

glanced toward the TV. "Looks like I missed the game. How'd it go?"

"The Lakers won. The other team had butterfingers."

"That must have been entertaining." He set down the mug and leaned back, resting his elbows on the bar.

His report didn't tally with the one-sided conversation Amy had heard him conduct before he left. "Okay, I give up," she said. "Who's Lucy and why did she and Tara and Greg ask you to drive an hour and a half to build a sand castle?"

"Not sand. Lego and, in Tara's case, blocks."

A glimmer of light shone at the end of the tunnel. "Some if not all of the aforementioned persons are children?"

"I'm sorry, I thought I'd told you about Tara and Greg. They're my niece and nephew," he said. "Their parents died a year ago and they live with Lucy. She's their aunt on their mother's side."

Amy resisted the urge to let out a whoop of joy. "You must be close to them."

"I try to be, although I haven't done a very good job," he said. "Greg burned his hand this morning and Lucy asked me to come check on it."

"How old is he?"

"Four," Quent said. "It wasn't serious, but the kids were so glad to see me, I couldn't leave. Besides, I enjoy being around them."

"You're good with young people," she said. "You were terrific with the Moms in Training. I was impressed."

"They're a great bunch." His expression sobered. "It's a shame they have to deal with adult problems when they're so young. Raising children is a big responsibility."

"Most new parents don't think about the future." In talking with the clinic's social worker, Amy had been surprised to learn that many new moms and dads didn't even put child-resistant locks on cabinets, as if they couldn't imagine their newborns becoming toddlers. "They figure if they know how to change a diaper, they've got it made."

"Changing diapers is hard. The nurses tell me I don't fasten them tight enough." Quent broke off and grimaced at the TV. "For heaven's sake, why is the sports channel showing ice-skating?"

"Because some people like to watch it." Amy's attention fixed on the screen. "Oh, look, it's part of the Grand Prix series."

"Doesn't that involve cars?" Quent asked hopefully.

"It's an international series of skating competitions." How could anyone not know that? she wondered.

Across the room, a couple of guys waved at Brian. "Change the channel!" one of them called. "Find some sports!"

"How about a martial arts movie?" added his buddy. "I'll settle for that."

"Can it, both of you!" Amy roared. "Ice-skating is also a sport. Get over it!"

They gave her dirty looks. "The lady's right!" Quent bellowed. "Stick a sock in it!"

"I guess you told 'em," Brian said, although he sounded dubious.

Amy glanced at Quent. "Thanks for the support."

"It can't hurt us to watch." Turning to Brian, he ordered a ham sandwich, one of the few food items available at the Paris Bar. "I'm trying to broaden my horizons."

"That's a good idea. I love ice-skating."

They sat in companionable silence. Outside, rain drummed on the roof, nearly drowning out the music and conversations.

Despite her usual enthusiasm for the sport, Amy quickly lost interest in what was on TV. All she could think about was Quent sitting beside her.

The image of him playing with children made him even more masculine, more desirable to her. She wished they could be alone together.

At her age, she ought to know a subtle way to persuade him to leave the bar and take her somewhere. Right now, though, she couldn't think of anything that wasn't embarrassingly blatant.

ALL THE LEAPING and spinning on TV couldn't compare to what was going on in Quent's nervous system. Being near Amy sensitized his entire body to every little movement she made.

Although his last couple of efforts at romance had petered out, this, Quent decided, was the perfect time to put his campaign into action. "Let's go dancing," he said.

Amy gave a start and nearly fell off her stool. "Did you say dancing?"

That wasn't a promising reaction. Quent refused to let it bother him. "There's a restaurant down by the water that has a band until 1:00 a.m. on weekends," he said. "Would you like to go?"

"I'd love to! I..." She glanced ruefully down at her jeans. "I'm afraid I'm not dressed for it. And I didn't bring any fancy stuff to my aunt's house."

Quent wasn't going to let a little detail like clothes stop them. "It's not far to your condo," he pointed out. "You could change."

He'd prefer it if they never even left the condo. But that wouldn't be romantic, he reminded himself.

"Done!" Amy said. "Besides, I want to see how my roof is holding up."

They swung their stools toward each other at the same moment and bumped knees. Through Amy's jeans, Quent could feel the shapely length of her legs. "Sorry," he muttered, although he wasn't.

"You get up first."

"My pleasure." Skimming to his feet, he caught her waist as Amy stood. Although she had no need of aid, she didn't object.

His palms registered the litheness of her toned muscles and the slimness of her midsection. Fire shot through Quent. With difficulty, he schooled his features into a pleasant mask and hurried to open the door for her.

Amy studied him uncertainly as she slipped by. Her pupils appeared slightly dilated, but perhaps that was a trick of the light.

He followed her car with his SUV. The burst of rain had softened to a persistent drizzle, and the wet pavement glimmered beneath his headlights.

When they arrived, Quent was glad to see that the property manager had done a good job. The tree was gone and the hole had been neatly boarded over.

Inside her living room, all appeared dry but disorderly. Bits of white ceiling lay everywhere and a musty smell arose from the carpet. "I've ordered new carpet and arranged to get the ceiling fixed," Amy told him. "Everything's on hold until the roof's done."

While she went into the bedroom, Quent stood listening to the rustling noises from the other room. He couldn't help picturing Amy stripping off her jeans and sweater.

Silence followed. She must be standing in front of the closet, choosing an outfit. Quent pictured her wearing the lingerie he'd seen in the drawer. Mostly, he imagined her bare waist, sculpted navel and those long legs.

He wished Amy would stroll out and pose sensuously in the doorway, wearing nothing but her bra and panties. If she gave him that sweet smile of hers, he'd be there in an instant to draw her against him.

This time, he wouldn't grope her like an overeager adolescent. He'd take it slow, pleasing her at every step, and, oh, she would certainly know how to please him.

To his embarrassment, Quent registered the fact that his pants had grown tight and his breath was coming fast. He went into the kitchen and stared at a Lakers' home game schedule on the refrigerator until he recovered.

A short time later, Amy appeared, a maroon sweater-dress clinging to her slim figure. Long dark hair flowed around her shoulders and she paused in the kitchen entrance just as he'd imagined, although with more clothes on. Quent moved toward her.

"It's stopped raining," she said. "Shall we take your car or mine?"

His instincts urged him to sweep her into his arms, but he knew Cary Grant would take her dancing first. "I'll drive," he said.

Amy grabbed a coat from the hall closet. "Come on, slowpoke!"

With a sigh for lost opportunities, Quent followed. Outside, the drizzle had ended. The moon peered through parting clouds and a few bold stars sparkled against slivers of blue-black sky.

In his SUV, they whipped down Pacific Coast Highway and pulled into the parking lot of the Sailor's Retreat, a seafood restaurant beside Serene Harbor. In front, an anchor mounted on a concrete block reflected the nautical theme.

Quent opened Amy's door. "This is different," she said as they walked toward the wood-shingled restaurant.

"They haven't changed anything as far as I can tell."

"Not the restaurant. The way you're acting. You held the door for me several times tonight." She shot him a questioning look. "Is this a date?"

"Would you mind if it were?" Quent asked.

She took a long breath. "No," she said. "Not at all."

Pleased, he escorted her inside, to the welcome lilt of a romantic melody. The earlier rain must have kept some customers at home, because the hostess agreed at once when Quent asked for a table near the dance floor.

Heads turned as Amy, radiantly beautiful and completely unselfconscious, crossed the room. Proudly, Quent held a chair for her and slid it forward when she sat down.

As they ordered drinks, her nearness hummed through him. The knit dress breathed with her, becoming part of her allure. Her hair, loose and dark around her expressive face, drove him crazy.

"You look amazing," Quent said.

Wariness shaded her eyes. "Amazing how?"

He smiled, touched by her lack of ego. "I've never met a woman who wrapped so many different personas into one. You're a tomboy, a professional woman and a siren, all at the same time."

"A siren?" she asked. "Me?"

On the verge of pointing out that men flocked to her, Quent made a quick mental right turn. He didn't care about those other men and he didn't want Amy to care about them, either. The growing intimacy between the two of them was the only thing that mattered.

"A man could get lost in your eyes," he said, staring into them in fascination. "They're so dark and honest."

She took in a shaky breath. "It's as if you can see right down inside me."

"I can, because of how well I know you." On the table, Quent cupped his hand across hers. The delicate bones fit beneath his palm like a small, vibrant bird. "While we've been getting to know each other as friends, something else has been happening. Something deeper."

Her lips parted, revealing a glistening hint of ivory and welcoming pink softness. "I feel it, too."

Their drinks arrived. This sense of hovering on the brink was so precious that Quent wanted to relish it for hours.

The orchestra segued into a sensuous Latin rhythm redolent of Brazilian beaches and tan, sunswept skin. Suddenly he could restrain himself no longer.

"Would you like to dance?" he asked.

"You bet." Amy stood up, taking Quent's arm. Her fresh scent drifted into his brain, intensifying his longing as they joined the other dancers on the floor.

The tantalizing beat engulfed them. Lights skimmed across Amy, revealing the invitation in her eyes and allure of her movements. She became the dance, infused with its voluptuousness.

The teasing quality to her smile lit fires inside Quent.

His body shifted closer, until their hips and shoulders brushed.

He knew where the dance was leading. And he wanted to go there so badly that if he held out much longer, he might burst into a column of flame.

Chapter Seven

Every time she and Quent touched, sparks of longing ignited inside Amy's most private places. She wanted more of him, all of him. She'd never experienced this intensity of desire for a man before, and she could hardly wait to discover where it would lead.

The other dancers barely registered in her mind. Like phantoms, they paled before her rising excitement.

When the music shifted into a waltz, she and Quent flowed into each other's arms. Her tilted head fitted comfortably inside the curve of his neck.

Amy heard his breath catch as her cheek grazed his jaw. With delicious awareness, she sensed a tightening in his body. Always before when she got close to a man, she'd become awkward and self-conscious. Not tonight.

She closed her eyes and let his scent of citrus and pure maleness simmer through her. Along his jawline, she detected a slight roughness, a reminder of untamed masculinity.

Warmth flowed from the point where his hand pressed her waist, while his other hand cradled hers as if to keep it safe. For the first time in her life, she wanted to yield utterly.

The music stopped. With one impulse, Amy and

Quent wove through the crowd toward a glass door that opened onto the restaurant's deck. Chill air raised bumps on her skin when they went out, but Quent's nearness seared it away.

Behind them, the door muffled the music. The deck lay empty, its round tables rain-washed. Shore lights glimmered against the smooth harbor and the fresh air carried the sea's wild tang.

The two of them sauntered down wooden steps to a quay just a few feet above the waterline. Hand-in-hand, they strolled away from the restaurant's long windows along a row of darkened shops. In this quiet place away from the world, they could be alone with the night.

As if they were still dancing, Amy turned and lifted her arms. Her foot slipped a little on the wet wood but Quent caught her and gathered her close.

When he kissed her, she felt as if she were floating. Then his tongue touched hers and desire flashed through her.

Amy gripped Quent's shoulders while liquid heat poured from his mouth into hers. Her body took his measure from the brush of their knees to his arousal, up to the point where the hard nubs of her breasts met his chest.

Quent drew his head back, his gaze questioning. Her fingers found the nape of his neck and urged him into another kiss.

After a moment, his mouth trailed from her mouth to her ear. The whisper of a breath in its sensitive coils nearly made her cry out. The restraints, the doubts, the fears of a lifetime vanished before this intense need. Amy cared for this man and wanted to be part of him.

"Let's go somewhere," she said.

He nodded, and they both spoke at once. "Your place."

Amy laughed. Since they had to make a choice, she said, "It doesn't matter. Surprise me," and stepped back.

She'd forgotten the slippery spot and her high heels. In one unguarded moment, her foot lost its traction and shot out from under her. Amy twisted backward, out of control.

She expected to thump to the boards and that would be the end of it, a silly tumble followed by an embarrassed scramble to her feet. But it didn't happen that way.

Momentum and gravity carried her backward into the railing. With a sickening sense of disbelief, she heard the wood splinter and felt it give way. Off-balance, she teetered on the brink of plunging into the cold water.

ALTHOUGH THE DISTANCE between Quent and Amy was slight, the milliseconds it took his brain to register the situation and his muscles to respond seemed like an eternity. Then, when he caught her arm, the impetus of her fall coupled with the unexpected failure of the railing made him misgauge the force needed, and he lost his grip.

Fighting panic, Quent lunged forward and grabbed her more tightly. At the same time, Amy clamped one hand over a post supporting another section of rail. Between the two of them, they pulled her to safety.

"That was close." She leaned over like a spent athlete, gasping for breath.

Quent's throat clamped. It took a moment before he could rasp out, "Are you all right?"

"My ankle's sore." Amy lifted it gingerly. "I don't think it's sprained, though."

He stood there stiffly, wanting to give her comfort and reassurance. But he couldn't move.

He'd almost lost Amy, and he hadn't even seen the danger coming. If she'd fallen, could he have saved her? The harbor was deceptively calm, but as a doctor, Quent knew people sometimes disappeared into a lake or the ocean and for no apparent reason never surfaced again.

It had nearly happened tonight. In a place where they'd felt perfectly safe, Amy could have been torn away.

The shock of that night a year ago rushed back. The phone jolting him from sleep, the disembodied voice of his father, the disorientation when he learned that three people he loved had been wiped from the earth.

Life could jerk the rug out from under you without warning. Until this moment, Quent hadn't realized how deep the trauma ran. He'd thought he was ready for the next step in his relationship with Amy. Unfortunately, he wasn't.

"I'd better take you back to your aunt's house," he said.

"My condo will be fine." She managed a shaky smile. "I never did lay in any more beer or popcorn, but I did pick up some coffee. And my car's there, remember?"

Quent took her arm and walked her slowly back to the restaurant. "You're shivering. I want your aunt to keep an eye on you. Someone can pick up your car in the morning."

"I'd rather you kept an eye on me," she said.

He didn't know how to answer because his reaction didn't make sense, even to him. Right now, it made him uneasy to be around Amy. As if he were cursed, as if what had happened tonight was his fault.

Or maybe because his losses had opened a wound that, far from healing, had lain festering all these months. He knew only that he couldn't bare his heart to Amy when it was still so raw.

"I just want you to be safe," he said, and took refuge in action. It was comforting to seize control of the situation by demanding to see the restaurant manager and telling the man in blunt terms what had happened.

"I'm so sorry. Are you all right, ma'am?" the man said. After Amy assured him that she was, he went on, "The quay is city property. I'll notify the authorities right away. They repaired part of the railing last summer but they must have missed some dry rot."

"I hate to think what would have happened if a child had tried to climb on it," Quent said.

"You're absolutely right," the man said. "I'll ask the city to send someone immediately to post the area with a no trespassing sign."

"Thank you." Amy tugged Quent's arm in a let's-go gesture.

"Are you sure you don't want to see a doctor?" the manager asked.

"I am a doctor," Quent said. "I'll take care of her."

After collecting Amy's coat, he escorted her to his SUV. "Did you mean that?" she said.

He paused in the act of closing her door. "Did I mean what?"

"About taking care of me?"

He knew only that he had a strong urge to protect her, even from himself. "Do you think you need medical attention?"

"Quent!"

"What?"

"Oh, get inside," she said.

He circled the vehicle and eased behind the wheel. "Where does your aunt live?"

"I can't believe you're really taking me there." Amy's eyes caught a sheen from a nearby streetlight. "I realize our mood got interrupted, but we can recapture it."

With her natural resilience, no doubt that was true for her. Normally, Quent could have, too. But right now he hardly knew his own mind.

He'd been raised to believe a man ought to be in control of himself. And he'd lost it out there, even if only for a moment. The results could have been fatal.

"You might suffer from delayed shock," he said, retreating into his intellect because it was easier than acknowledging his emotions. "That was a close call."

"You make it sound so clinical," she said.

He put the vehicle into gear and backed up. "You haven't given me your aunt's address yet."

"Don't shut me out like this!" Amy said.

"I can't help it." That was as much of an explanation as he could offer.

She waited a moment to give him a chance to say more, but he didn't. At last, she broke the silence. "Aunt Mary lives off Alsace Avenue." She provided the address. "Do you know where that is?"

"Yes." He'd learned the geography of Serene Beach after he moved here by tacking up street maps in the bathroom. He'd used the same tactic to memorize anatomy charts in medical school.

Quent turned east onto the highway and steered toward a large development of middle-class homes. He knew he ought to say more, but how could he explain what he didn't fully understand?

"I don't get it," Amy said. "All of a sudden you're not even talking to me?"

"I'm not usually like this, I know," Quent admitted. "But there's another side to me."

"Was one of your ancestors a clam?" she teased, trying to lighten the tone of their conversation. "Is that what you haven't told me?"

With an effort, he smiled. "I come from a long line of mollusks."

"Enough joking. You're dodging the issue." She folded her arms.

"Okay, I admit it. I don't want to talk about this tonight." His chest ached. He must have strained a muscle when he lunged toward her on the quay. "Can we go back to being friends for a while? I'm afraid I pushed things too far too fast."

"I don't think you pushed them far enough," she said wistfully.

In the back of his mind, Quent heard the Latin beat and saw Amy dancing like a temptress as her dark eyes bored into his. Although his body tightened at the memory, it seemed to come from another lifetime.

Maybe he simply wasn't ready to take the next step from closeness to true intimacy. In the heat of the moment, he hadn't thought beyond the joy of coupling and the early, glorious days of mutual discovery.

His parents' relationship had shown him how love could warp under the pressure of commitment. What must once have been a passionate union had deteriorated into a cold war. If it could happen to them, why not to him and Amy?

"Let's take it slow. Maybe we can play a few rounds of laser tag next week," Quent said.

"I can't. Natalie and Patrick's wedding is Saturday and I'm one of the bridesmaids, remember?" Amy watched him thoughtfully. "You know I'm not going to let up until you tell me what grim thoughts are churning around inside that blond head of yours."

"You're welcome to try," Quent said. "But I'm not much for plumbing the depths of my psyche, Counselor."

"'Physician, heal thyself,'" she quoted.

"I'm trying," he said. "Time heals all wounds, doesn't it?"

"I'm not so sure."

"I'll see you at work Monday. We'll sort this out eventually."

It was the best he could do, and she was going to have to accept it. Besides, they'd reached her aunt's house.

Quent escorted Amy to the door and saw her inside. He wished he could take her upstairs and tuck her into bed himself, bring her a cup of hot chocolate and make sure she was all right.

But he wanted to reestablish their distance until these confusing feelings subsided. Surely things would work themselves out, if they could both be patient.

At least they were still friends.

AMY SLEPT POORLY and, exhausted, dozed late the next morning. In her dreams, she kept falling. Each time, Quent tried to catch her, but at the last moment, he would disappear or lose his grip.

Darn him, she thought when she awoke with her eyes stinging and her throat dry. She was the one who'd nearly gotten dumped into the drink, not him. Why was he making such a fuss?

Maybe because the two of you were getting closer than he wanted.

She pulled the quilt around her and stared grumpily at the ceiling. This wasn't the first time she and Quent had gotten physical, and each time fate had intervened. Even so, nobody, not even her own brain, was going to tell her the man didn't want to sleep with her.

She needed an objective opinion. This fall, when her friend Natalie had discovered she was pregnant and needed to decide how to break the news to Patrick, she'd come to Amy for advice. It was time to turn the tables.

Besides, Natalie was almost a married woman. Maybe she'd have some plum words of wisdom.

By the time Amy took a shower and called her friend, it was after noon. "How about a late brunch?" Natalie asked. "Patrick and I ate early and I'm ready for another meal."

That sounded great, until Amy remembered that Natalie wasn't living in her cozy apartment anymore. A few weeks ago, she'd moved into her fiancé's mansion.

Amy wasn't sure she wanted to spill her deepest troubles within hearing of the hospital administrator. "What I need to discuss is private. If Patrick's going to be around, let's meet somewhere else."

"Don't worry." Natalie's flat, down-to-earth voice dispelled Amy's lingering trace of uneasiness. "He's in his home office, getting ahead on paperwork so we can enjoy our honeymoon."

"I'll be there in fifteen minutes. And I'm starving, so I'll take you up on the food offer."

"Fantastic!"

Amy was halfway down the stairs before she remembered that she'd left her car at the condo. "Aunt Mary?" she called, and waited. There was no answer.

Apparently Mary and Kitty—and the family van—were still at church. With a sigh, Amy marched into the hall to call a cab. She was reaching for the directory when she spotted a note propped against her pocketbook, which she'd left on a chair.

Hope you're feeling better. I took Kitty to your condo early this a.m. and she drove your car home. I figured you'd be needing it.

Love,
Aunt Mary.

The keys were sitting on the chair beside her purse.

How sweet! Her aunt had been concerned last night when she'd learned of the mishap, but Amy hadn't expected anything like this.

Gratefully, she wrote notes of thanks to each of them. Then she drove to Natalie's house.

On the radio, the forecaster called for more rain. Oh, well, it suited her mood.

The Barr mansion was located directly behind Doctors Circle, which had originally been built on part of the Barr estate. The house, secluded behind graceful landscaping, lay across St. Michel Way from the Birthing Center.

The mansion presented an image of classical grandeur, with its front portico, elegant lines and modern expanses of glass. Steering along the curved drive, Amy enjoyed the view past the swimming pool and across the bluffs. Below stretched Paris Avenue and, beyond it, Pacific Coast Highway and the harbor.

She shivered, remembering again that plunge across

the quay and the helpless sensation as the railing broke beneath her. But Quent had been there. It had felt wonderful, being pulled into the warmth of his arms.

Why had he withdrawn so abruptly? Even now, after a night spent consciously and subconsciously reviewing everything that had happened, Amy didn't understand.

When it came to her own predicament, her counseling training was useless. She hoped Natalie could provide some insight.

Her friend opened the door as Amy mounted the steps. Pregnancy and happiness made her bloom. Her blond hair appeared thicker than ever, her skin was velvety and her blue eyes shone. At four months along, her abdomen formed a healthy mound beneath her calf-length blue cotton dress.

"I just fried more bacon, so hurry before it gets cold!" she said, as if the mouthwatering scent filling the air hadn't already given away the menu. "And don't tell Heather what I'm eating. I'm sure bacon isn't on the nutrition list."

"It's fine with me," Amy said as she scurried inside. "I need comfort food."

"Whatever's bothering you, it must be bad. When you're upset, I've noticed that you tend to binge on junk food," Natalie said as they crossed the marbled foyer. A circular staircase rose to their right while, at the back, the foyer opened into a sunken living room.

"Doesn't everybody?" Amy asked.

"When I'm upset, I hug my stuffed bunny. Or I used to. Now I hug Patrick."

Amy wished she could turn to Quent when she was upset. Unfortunately, he was the cause of her problems, not the solution.

"You're sure Patrick's in his office?" she asked. "This is really, really personal."

"He's buried up to his neck. I've warned him, no paperwork, no laptop, no e-mail, no phone calls on our honeymoon." The pair planned a Caribbean cruise. "We'll be working late every night this week, but it's worth it."

"I can imagine," Amy said.

"Mostly I think he's worried about the Endowment Fund," Natalie confided, lowering her voice. "It was a noble idea to raise thirty million dollars by May and assure the future of Doctors Circle, but he may have been overly optimistic. We're only up to ten million."

"That sounds like a lot to me," Amy said.

"It's only a third of the goal," her friend said. "Well, there's time left. Lots of things can happen between now and May."

They strolled into the kitchen. Cheerful even on an overcast day, it provided a splendid view of the bluffs and the ocean. With its generous cabinet and counter space and a center island, it provided enough room for even the most ambitious cook.

On one wall, an assortment of china rabbits filled a knickknack shelf. Below, another shelf displayed coffee mugs and a teapot decorated with bunnies. Natalie had been collecting them for years.

The two women perched at the round table, which was set with Peter Rabbit china. Muffins peeked from a napkin-covered basket. Scrambled eggs, bacon and, of course, coffee completed the meal.

"This is fabulous," Amy said. "I feel better already."

"I'm honored that the counselor has come to me for advice," Natalie teased as they dug in.

"You were my first choice." Amy wished briefly that she could confide in her mother. Although she'd long ago reestablished a friendly relationship with her mom, Frieda, being abandoned at the age of twelve was a difficult obstacle to overcome.

"Well?" Natalie finished buttering a muffin. "Don't keep me in suspense!"

"It's Quent," Amy said. "I can't figure him out." She sketched last night's events, including his abrupt emotional withdrawal. "It was as if I hit a wall. I don't even know why. Did we really go too far too fast? Did he get jolted out of his daze and realize he'd nearly made a big mistake? Or was it my clumsiness that put him off?"

"I'm no genius at figuring out men," Natalie admitted, her expression rueful. "My first marriage was a disaster."

"You were young," Amy said. "I'm thirty-three. What's my excuse?"

"You can take pride in your accomplishments," Natalie said. "It's not your fault you haven't found the right guy."

"Or I've found him and lost him," she said sadly.

"I'll bet he got cold feet." Natalie poured them each a second cup of coffee. "You're too much woman for him."

The remark startled a laugh from Amy. "I wish!"

"Honestly, you've got blinders on," her friend said. "Men practically keel over when you walk by."

"It's the paint fumes."

"No, it's because you're beautiful and smart, even if you don't realize it," Natalie pressed. "Take Rob Sentinel. He practically steps on his tongue every time he sees you."

"Oh, come on." Amy liked the new obstetrician but she hadn't had much contact with him. "He's a good-looking guy. I'm sure he has more female companionship than he knows what to do with."

"I'll tell you what," Natalie said. "Give Quent a rest. If he wants to put some distance between you, that's his problem. Go out with other guys."

Amy considered this advice while finishing her bacon and eggs. Occasionally she got asked out by some guy or other that she met while jogging or at the Paris Bar, but none of them had made much of an impression. "There isn't anybody I want to go out with."

"What about Rob?"

"He's never asked me," she said.

"The way you always hang out with Quent, he probably thinks you're taken," Natalie said. "I'll tell you what. Friday night, we're having an informal rehearsal dinner at Patrick's sister's house. She won't mind if you invite Rob as your escort."

Amy hadn't asked a guy out since she got negative feedback in high school, but that had been a long time ago. And although she hadn't felt any sparks toward Rob, he was undeniably good-looking. "It might seem odd, coming out of the blue."

"Make it casual," Natalie advised. "Since he's new, suggest it'll give him a chance to get to know people better. If he says no, what have you lost?"

Quent had said he wanted to go back to being friends. It might make him more comfortable if he knew she was going out with other men, Amy supposed. "You're sure Patrick's sister won't mind an extra guest?"

"Bernie's an inveterate matchmaker," Natalie said. "She practically threw me and Patrick together. She'll be thrilled to have you bring a date."

"It's worth a try," Amy agreed. Putting some psychological distance between herself and Quent was a good idea. In any case, she thought, it couldn't hurt. "I'll ask him tomorrow."

She was pleased to discover that the decision calmed her. At the very least, it gave her something to focus on beyond Quent's puzzling behavior.

Maybe the sense-memory of his touch while they were dancing and the whisper of his breath in the coil of her ear would finally fade. But she wasn't banking on it.

Chapter Eight

"Okay, now, this doesn't count," Quent said as he carried the basket of cookie flowers into Amy's office on Monday.

It was a new item he'd spotted this morning at the Birthing Center gift shop, and he hadn't been able to resist. Shaped and iced to resemble tulips, the giant cookies rose on sticks around a heart-shaped cookie traced with the words, "Congratulations!"

Amy regarded him with an endearing expression of puzzlement that made his heart perform loop-the-loops. Darn, but he'd missed her in the past two days!

"What are you congratulating me for?" she asked. "And what do you mean, it doesn't count?"

"I'm congratulating you on your close escape from falling into the drink," he said. "And it doesn't count as a romantic gesture."

That whole campaign had been a mistake, he'd concluded. This yearning to make fiery love to Amy carried within it the seeds of destruction of the best relationship in his life.

"Okay, you've cleared up the first point," she said. "Now, what's wrong with romantic gestures?"

"They lead to romance." Quent set the basket on her desk. It livened up the room, in his opinion.

"And what, pray tell, is wrong with romance?" Amy asked.

"It doesn't last," he said. "Friendship does."

"They're not mutually exclusive."

"How many couples do you know who've managed to maintain a long-term love affair without eventually becoming alienated?" he challenged. He already knew her parents' marriage had been a disaster, so surely she would understand.

Amy's hands made graceful patterns in the air as she searched for an answer. She'd once told him it was part of her Italian heritage to talk as much with gestures as with words. "Well, there's…" She stopped, stymied.

"My point exactly," Quent said. "Now, how many people do you know who've remained friends for decades?"

She wrinkled her nose. "Several. But they're people of the same sex, or colleagues who work together."

"Like us."

"Quent, are you going to deny what we both feel?" Amy demanded.

"The more we feel, the more precious it is," he said, "and the more I want to preserve it." Since she made no move to help herself, he plucked one of the tulip cookies from the basket and handed it to her. "These are meant to be eaten."

"I'm willing to take the risk," she said as if she hadn't heard.

"I'm not." Right now, Quent had an almost irresistible impulse to swing around Amy's desk and kiss her. He stopped himself.

He still hadn't sorted through the dark feelings roused

by Saturday night's near-accident. Confronting painful emotions wasn't part of his upbringing and it jarred him. He just wanted to get back to normal, which meant having fun with Amy, no strings attached.

Giving in, she took a bite out of the cookie. "It's delicious. These are all for me, I presume."

"You aren't sharing?" Tasting them was half the point of the purchase.

"I think sharing is awfully romantic," Amy said. "Therefore you wouldn't be interested."

"Friends share, too."

"Friends don't give presents, then keep half for themselves." After a somber moment, she burst out laughing. "You should see your face! Disappointment is written all over it."

"Does this mean you aren't serious?" Quent asked hopefully.

"It's hard to be serious around you. Go ahead, take one. But only one," Amy warned.

Quent chose a luscious red flower. It tasted of sugar and spice with just the right degree of crunchiness. "It's excellent." As he ate, his gaze fell on four photographs mounted on the wall. The colorful images of children and babies at play reminded him of his niece and nephew. "Those are new, aren't they?"

"What do you think of them?"

"Thumbs up." He finished the cookie and tossed the stick into the wastebasket. "You must really like kids."

"Of course," Amy said. "You knew that."

"No, I didn't." The discovery pleased him. Maybe soon they could both drive down and visit his niece and nephew, Quent thought.

"Do you want another one?" she asked.

"Another what?" Images of children danced through his mind.

"I can't believe there are cookies in the room and you're thinking about something else," Amy said.

"Oh, that." He no longer cared about the cookies. He was too busy imagining Tara and Greg nestling into Amy's arms. "No, thanks. I'd better head back to the clinic before Dudley shows up to lecture me. I just came to say hello."

"And bring me a present," Amy reminded him. "Thank you."

"You're welcome." There was so much more he wanted to give her. As a friend, of course, he told himself, and went back to work.

AMY DIDN'T UNDERSTAND Quent. Over the next few days, he behaved almost like his old self, yet whenever they happened to touch, he pulled back. He was protecting himself, she supposed. Perhaps, in a way, he was protecting her, too.

Although Amy would have given almost anything to recapture the tenderness they'd experienced on Saturday night, doubts crept in. Maybe Quent was right. She had no experience with sustaining relationships. What made her think she could hold on to a guy as devastatingly attractive as he was?

Being friends meant something special to them both. Maybe it could be enough.

On Wednesday, she got some good news. A high-pressure system moved in and the long-delayed roofers were finally able to start. She was told the roof should be fixed by the following week, so Amy scheduled the interior work to begin on her condo.

Wednesday also marked her first counseling session

with Cynthia Hernandez, Heather's nurse. The young woman's mood was more cheerful than it had been the previous week, mostly because Heather had returned to work.

She poured out her story to a sympathetic Amy. Earlier in the year, Cynthia had begun dating a man, only to learn later that he was married. By that time, she was pregnant—with twins.

Even though she knew she'd been tricked, Cynthia had a hard time accepting that her boyfriend wasn't going to leave his wife and take care of her. Amy encouraged her to talk about her emotionally abusive father and to see the similarities to her boyfriend. Pleased at the insight, Cynthia scheduled another session for the following week.

By Friday, Amy was more than ready for the weekend break. She'd been racing around yesterday and today, checking on her new roof and paying for it when the work was finished, which had happened that afternoon.

To complicate matters, she hadn't slept well all week. Her brain kept replaying Saturday's fiasco, trying to make it come out differently. And failing.

The result was a stretched-out, light-headed sensation. Maybe that was why, as she prepared to leave work on Friday, the babies and children on the wall laughed and tumbled so vividly that she could almost hear their little voices. Merry eyes seemed to fix on her longingly.

It was like a dream come to life. They were so sweet, she wished they were hers.

You must really like kids. Quent had thrown out the comment so casually that, at the time, it had scarcely registered.

Now tears blurred Amy's vision. She wanted so much to hold a baby in her arms! A child of her own, someone who needed her. Someone who belonged to her.

This was irrational, Amy scolded herself. She wasn't even married and might never be. It must be the prospect of Natalie's wedding that made her so emotional.

She went out, locked the door and leaned against it. Her heart was pounding and her throat felt dry. This was crazy. No, this was what people called her biological clock, ticking overtime in spite of her best intentions.

"Is something wrong?" She hadn't heard Quent approach until he spoke.

"I guess I'm a little overexcited about the wedding rehearsal tonight," she said.

"Do you need a hug?"

More than he knew! "Is that the pediatrician's favorite prescription?"

"It works wonders." Quent pulled her against his shoulder. "Tell your troubles to Dr. Ladd."

"What if my trouble *is* Dr. Ladd?" Amy hadn't meant to say anything so revealing. "Just kidding. All I need is to shift gears and get ready for tonight's events."

"There's more than one?" he asked.

"There's a dinner at Patrick's sister's house after the rehearsal." She found herself reluctant to mention that Rob Sentinel was escorting her. As Natalie had predicted, the soft-spoken obstetrician had accepted her invitation immediately.

Although Amy liked him, she had no desire to nestle against him as she was doing now with Quent. Pushing aside her reflections, she took several deep breaths.

Quent smelled like home, she mused happily. And like safety.

But the impression was illusory. Even the curve of his arm closing around her, holding her in place, was only the support of a friend.

Regretfully, Amy slipped away. "I'd better go or I'll be late."

"We can't have that." He watched her thoughtfully. "I'm afraid I've got to work."

"Maybe I'll see you at the wedding tomorrow."

"I'll wave as you go down the aisle," he said.

Outside, Amy drove home beneath a spectacular pink sunset that transformed Serene Beach into a fairyland. She wished Quent were here to see it.

Rob Sentinel arrived at Aunt Mary's door promptly at six-thirty. The young obstetrician looked darkly attractive in his suit, and Amy wished she could experience something stronger than admiration.

In his early thirties, Rob had an air of confidence and a ready smile, but there was something reserved about him, too. Perhaps it was the scar on one cheek that gave him an air of mystery.

In the car, they talked about Heather's return to work. Rob, who'd been taking care of her patients while building up a caseload of his own, was glad his colleague had returned.

The rehearsal took place at the Serenity Fellowship Church, located next to Doctors Circle. Amy was touched that Patrick had not only chosen his brother-in-law, advertising executive Mike Lincoln, as his best man, but also his two young nephews as his ushers.

The minister outlined the service, the choirmaster told them when the hymns would be sung, and the bridal party walked through their roles. Then they left for Mike and Bernie Barr Lincoln's house in Serene Cove.

"I hadn't seen this part of town before," Rob said as they drove between harborside luxury homes. "It's impressive."

"I've never been here before, either."

They fell silent. Amy suspected there was a deep mind at work beneath Rob's low-key manner, and under other circumstances he might be a fascinating conversationalist, but it would take the right woman to bring him out. Tonight had demonstrated to her satisfaction that she was not that woman.

Inside the Lincolns' multi-level home, caterers had set up a sumptuous buffet. In addition to the wedding party, Patrick and Natalie had invited several out-of-town guests and close friends.

Their hostess, Patrick's sister Bernie, bubbled with good spirits as she greeted her guests. A vivacious young woman whose curly brown hair showed flashes of red-gold, she clearly enjoyed making everyone feel at home.

Amy was glad to see Rob become absorbed in talking to Mike. Although he might not excel at small talk, her date did know how to connect with people.

"Well?" Natalie asked her when they met by the coffee server. "How's it going?"

"Fine," she said.

"No heaving bosom? No rocketing pulse?"

"Nowhere close," Amy told her.

Natalie pretended to pout. "Who am I going to throw my bouquet to?"

"Not me!" said Heather, who was pouring herself a cup of decaf.

"Not me, either," Natalie's sister Candy chimed in from where she stood nearby. "I like being single."

"I'll take it," volunteered Angie, Natalie's mother. "I wouldn't mind getting married again."

As Candy and Natalie teased their mother about her latest boyfriend, a long-haired carpenter named Clovis who was making short work of the dessert offerings, Amy rejoined Rob by the buffet table. She wanted to make sure he had a good time, since he was her guest. "How're you doing?"

"Mike was telling me about his latest advertising campaign. I'm surprised Doctors Circle hasn't made more use of his talents," Rob said. "He could be a major resource for the Endowment Fund campaign."

"That's a good idea," Amy said. "You should send Patrick an e-mail and suggest it, although obviously he won't be doing anything about it right away."

"Why not?" Rob said.

"He's going to be on his honeymoon."

"Oh, right."

At this point, she'd have been poking Quent in the ribs and giving him a hard time about forgetting such an important event. With Rob, she didn't dare crack a joke for fear of looking foolish.

That was when, on the far side of the expansive living room, Amy spotted Quent, holding a couple of packages. Even in a crowd, he caught her attention instantly. What a relief! Nothing felt right without him.

It took a moment before she realized he wasn't alone. In fact, he was riveted on the stunning blond woman at his side.

Who was she? And, come to think of it, why had Quent showed up at an event he had no business attending? Amy wished all these other people would go away so she could give him a piece of her mind.

WHAT WAS Amy doing with Rob Sentinel? It was possible they'd simply run into each other by the buffet table, but something in Rob's stance gave Quent the impression he took a protective interest in her.

Beside him, the blonde continued talking. She'd explained when they arrived on the doorstep at the same time that she was Natalie's oldest sister.

"I flew down from Oregon as a surprise," Alana was saying as she accepted a glass of champagne from a passing waiter. "My mother and I don't see eye-to-eye, and I'm not close to my sisters, although I did lend Nat my wedding dress. My husband said if I missed the big day, I'd always regret it, so here I am."

"You can't skip an event like this." Inspired to elaborate, Quent added, "Families feud for generations over less. In fact, I think that's how the Hatfields and the McCoys got started. Somebody missed a wedding reception, and the next thing you know, they were shooting each other."

The remark tickled her. "My gosh, you have a funny way of putting things. I'll bet your patients love you."

"Mostly they're too young to get my jokes." Quent wondered why he couldn't catch Amy's gaze. He was almost certain she'd seen him come in. "Of course, I charm the pants off their parents."

Alana burst into giggles. "I'd like to see that!"

Was Amy purposely ignoring him? She'd been cuddly enough this afternoon, although, come to think of it, she had peeled away rather quickly. Had he done something to tick her off without realizing it?

Natalie, emerging from the kitchen, interrupted his

thoughts with a shriek. "I don't believe it! Alana! You came!" She tore across the room into her sister's arms.

Candy started screaming, too, and their mother approached somewhat less noisily. As other guests turned to look, Quent seized his chance to slip over to the buffet table.

Amy greeted him with an inquisitive arch of the brow. "I didn't realize you knew Natalie's sister. She's very pretty."

"We're old pals," he said. "We met five minutes ago."

He could have sworn he saw relief in her eyes. Well, good. If she'd been jealous, he'd laid her fears to rest. Now he needed to clear up what she was doing with Rob.

Before he could ask, she said, "What brings you to the rehearsal dinner? No offense, but I'm surprised to see you here, since you aren't in the wedding party."

"I'm surprised, too," Quent admitted. "I wasn't exactly invited. In fact, I wasn't invited at all."

"Now, this is an explanation I'd like to hear," Rob said.

Quent explained that he'd been working late when a deliveryman poked his nose into the Well-Baby Clinic. The man had a delivery to make to Dr. Barr's office but that building was locked tight.

Since the parcels appeared to be wedding gifts, Quent had signed for them and decided to bring them to Mrs. Lincoln's house tonight. He chose not to mention that the prime attraction had been the knowledge that Amy was attending the dinner.

"It's a good thing the Lincolns are listed in the phone book," he said. "I took it as a sign that they wouldn't mind me barging in. Was that pushy of me?"

"Definitely cheeky." Amy indicated the packages. "You should give those to Natalie as soon as she stops hollering and jumping up and down."

"My intention precisely." Since Dr. Barr had come within earshot, Quent turned to him and joked, "The clinic doesn't pay enough, so I've taken a second job as a deliveryman. This stuff is heavy! And I doubt you'll even give me a tip."

"What kind of tip did you have in mind, doctor?" Patrick joked.

"I suspect a plateful of food wouldn't hurt," Rob said. "The man looks famished to me."

The groom relieved Quent of his burden. "Help yourself. And thanks for bringing these."

"It was on my way." Quent kept a straight face through this obvious untruth, since Serene Cove, located on a slip of land that thrust into the ocean, wasn't on the way to anywhere.

"Well, we can always use more gifts," Patrick deadpanned in return, since everyone knew he'd inherited a house already filled with furniture and kitchenware. "I hope there's another blender in there. You can't have too many of those."

Quent wanted to stick around just in case Rob and Amy wanted company. Or, especially, in case they didn't. However, he really was hungry, and Rob had left him with no excuse to linger.

"I'm going to eat, now that I've been formally invited," he said. "Anyone care to join me?"

"I'm full," Rob said. "How about you, Amy?"

"Me, too. Help yourself, Quent," she said.

As he took a plate and made his way along the table, Quent faced the truth. Since there was no reason for

Rob to have received his own invitation tonight, the two of them must have come together.

He glanced back at them. They made a handsome couple, but he didn't want them to be a couple. Still, he couldn't blame the guy. If anyone knew how irresistible Amy could be, it was Quent.

If only he hadn't reacted so strongly last Saturday...yet he hadn't been able to help it. He simply wasn't ready to open his heart to Amy.

All the same, he didn't see how he could bear to lose her to somebody else.

Chapter Nine

Amy was glad she'd invited Rob to the rehearsal dinner. He'd had a good time, and so had she. But it had bothered her, seeing Quent's confused expression when she took Rob's arm and walked away.

More than confused. Hurt.

Later that night, she tossed restlessly in bed, wondering if she'd misread him. He wanted to keep her at arm's length, didn't he? Then why had he seemed so disappointed?

She didn't understand him. Maybe if she'd had more serious relationships, she would be able to figure Quent out. Even her Ph.D. in psychology didn't help, darn it.

Oh, the heck with it! she told herself sometime after midnight. Worrying didn't suit her. Let Quent take care of his own problems. If he wanted to talk to her, he could do it in his own sweet time.

She was not going to give it another thought. Absolutely not, Amy thought, and turned over on her stomach.

Finally, her face half-buried in the pillow, she fell into a much-needed sleep. By the time she awoke, sunlight was streaming through the window.

Her first thought as she blinked awake was, Oh, good! It's a pretty day for Nat's wedding!

Then she checked the bedside clock. Eleven-oh-seven. No, not possible. It must have stopped last night or gotten screwed up somehow.

Amy groped for her watch. It took a moment to focus on those tiny hour and minute hands.

Eleven-oh-eight. No question about it.

She bolted out of bed, wishing she could turn back time. The wedding started at one o'clock. As a bridesmaid, she was supposed to meet Natalie and the others at the church by noon.

Amy could have sworn she'd set the alarm for seven. But, as a teenager, she'd been infamous for her ability to sleep through buzzes, beeps and loud music. Obviously, she hadn't lost the knack.

After grabbing her robe and some underwear, she dashed down the hall to the bathroom. By luck, Kitty wasn't hogging the shower as she sometimes did. In fact, there was no sign of either her cousin or her aunt.

Getting ready in a hurry made Amy clumsy. The bar of soap slipped and slid into the tub. The shampoo stung her eyes. And, once she got out, her long hair took forever to dry.

Amy said a silent prayer of thanks that they'd chosen hats. As a result, she planned to wear her hair loose, so there was no need to fuss with putting it up.

The turquoise dress came with a sewn-in slip, which helped. Her panty hose ripped when Amy tried to yank them into place, but, thank heavens, she had a spare. The silver sandals went on smoothly, and she grabbed her gloves and her purse, ready to go.

It was five past noon. She'd be a few minutes late, but Natalie would understand, Amy thought as she swept down the stairs while groping inside her pocket-book for her car keys.

No keys.

Oh, come on. They had to be here!

Her fingers probed between tissues, breath mints, her cell phone, her brush and lipstick, but found no keys. What on earth had she done with them?

Amy dashed into the kitchen to dump out the contents on the table. She stopped when she spotted a neatly handwritten note at her place. It read:

Dear Amy,
I hope you don't mind me borrowing your car. You were sleeping and I didn't want to wake you. My mom's gone for the day and my friend called. Her parents' car won't start and her grandmother's arriving at the airport.
I'll be back as soon as I can.

Love,
Kitty

Amy groaned. Obviously, Kitty had forgotten the wedding was today. She'd run off to do a good deed, which was admirable, but she hadn't even indicated what time she might be back or which airport she was going to. There were several in the Los Angeles area, from twenty minutes to more than an hour's drive away.

Amy couldn't wait. She'd have to call a cab, although the last time she'd done that, it had taken forty minutes to arrive.

As she picked up her cell phone, she remembered that Quent lived only ten minutes from here and was planning to attend the service. It *was* an emergency, after all.

When she heard his brisk, ''Dr. Ladd'' on the phone, Amy was glad she'd called him. Just the sound of his voice reassured her.

''It's me.'' She sketched the situation. ''Can you give me a ride? I'd really appreciate it.''

''I'll get there as fast as I can.''

After hanging up, Amy called Nat and told her what had happened. ''I'll be at the church before one,'' she said. ''I'm sorry about the delay.''

''In a way, it makes me feel better,'' her friend said. ''Things were going too smoothly. I figured there had to be some kind of foul-up today, sort of a wedding jinx. Now it's arrived and it isn't bad.''

''Thanks, Nat. I won't let you down!''

Amy double-checked her appearance in the hall mirror. The turquoise dress suited her dark coloring and the hat gave her an unfamiliar air of elegance. She scarcely recognized herself.

A couple of people over the years had suggested that, with her height and cheekbones, she ought to be a model, but she'd figured they were hallucinating. Now she could kind of see their point, although she would never have the patience to pose for hours in front of a camera.

Oh, who was she kidding? Being tall and slim didn't make you a model. You had to be beautiful, too.

Amy made a face at herself in the mirror. She was just her plain old self, nothing more and nothing less. Besides, she enjoyed helping people through her work and she doubted she'd ever get that much satisfaction from standing around preening.

The jangle of the doorbell made her jump. How did he get here so fast? she wondered as she went to let him in.

With his blond hair still wet from the shower, Quent looked so sexy he set her pulse racing. Beneath his open suit jacket, the tailored blue shirt clung to a damp spot on his flat stomach, highlighting the breadth of his chest and the narrowness of his hips. Amy almost dared to reach out and button the coat for him, but she was afraid she might start undoing his shirt instead.

He gave a low whistle as he regarded her. "What a knockout!"

"It's the hat," Amy said. "And the color. Aren't they terrific?"

"Not to mention the woman who's wearing them," Quent replied. "But if you say so, of course, it's the hat that bowled me over."

His kidding restored her confidence. When he opened the door and took her elbow to help her step up into his SUV, Amy refrained from cracking a joke about not being a helpless old lady yet.

"If you keep this up, I might let you whisk me away to Paris," she teased. "Like one of my many boyfriends."

Quent's mouth twitched, but she couldn't tell whether he was almost smiling or almost frowning. "Did Rob invite you on a trip?"

"Rob?" she asked. "When would he find time to take a break? And please start the car! I'm in a hurry."

"Sorry." He got behind the wheel and pulled onto the road. "The way you said that, I wondered if you had a specific boyfriend in mind."

Amy couldn't believe the suspicion that cropped up. "Don't tell me you're jealous!"

"Of course not."

"I was," she admitted.

Quent cast her a droll look. "Care to tell me who inspired this unwarranted emotion?"

"Natalie's sister," Amy said. "The luscious blonde."

"You mean the chatterbox?"

She laughed. "Perspectives vary, I see."

"Now that we're 'fessing up, I'll admit I was wondering how you came to attend the party with Rob." Quent zipped through the light Saturday traffic.

"Natalie put me up to inviting him," Amy admitted. "I'm glad I did." Hearing no response, she explained, "He met lots of new people and I think it helped him feel more comfortable at Doctors Circle. Not everyone is as outgoing as you are."

"No sparks?" Quent asked. "No bongo drums thrumming in the background? No sweaty palms?"

"Especially no sweaty palms." He *had* been jealous! Outside, Amy could have sworn she heard birds singing.

She almost wished they weren't going to a wedding. She wanted to walk on the beach with Quent and dig her toes into the sand. They could buy fried clams at a snack shack and carry them to her condo, nice and snug now that she had a new roof. They wouldn't even have to worry about getting sand in the carpet, since it was going to be replaced next week.

Quent careened into the church parking lot and halted in front of the double doors. "Delivering you as promised, milady," he said.

"Thank you." Impulsively, Amy leaned over to kiss him. Her hat bumped his head, startling them both. As she reached to adjust it, Quent pulled her close and kissed her with lingering sweetness.

She melted like chocolate in the sun. All she wanted

was to taste his mouth, to feel his strong hands tighten on her waist, to go home with Quent and forget everything else.

Someone thumped on the glass and they sprang apart. Amy felt her cheeks grow hot. "Who was that?" She peered outside, but their tormenter had already gone into the church.

"I guess this is kind of a public place," Quent said. "I'm glad we did that, though."

"Me, too." Her blood racing, Amy hurried outside and into the foyer.

In a side room, she found the bride, breathtaking in a storybook white gown and a hat trimmed with feathers. The high waist and flowing skirt not only reinforced the impression of old-fashioned charm, they also disguised her pregnancy.

With their different heights and coloring, Heather and Candy each brought an individual sense of style to the turquoise dress. Angie had opted for a silver mother-of-the-bride suit adorned with a blue-green scarf.

"I'm sorry I'm late," Amy told them all. "My car went on a mission of mercy."

"All's well that ends well," Natalie said.

"We heard Quent was bringing you," Heather added. "How's that going?"

"How's what going?" Amy asked.

"Oh, come on!" Candy scoffed. "He practically tripped over his feet getting to you at the dinner last night. I was afraid for a minute he might deck that guy you brought."

"Quent was in a hurry to reach the food," Amy said. "He worked the late shift, which meant he was starving."

"I don't believe a word of it." Angie gave her

daughter a broad wink. "Throw her the bouquet. Take my word for it. She'll be the next to marry."

At last the bride shooed them all into the empty vestibule. Candy stuck her head into the sanctuary and signaled the organist that they were ready.

Although she'd known the church's choir was going to sing today, Amy hadn't been prepared for the swelling impact of voices as they launched into the processional. Thank goodness Candy was going first, because she needed a moment to clear her eyes.

Heather went second, followed by Amy. The airy church had been transformed into a fairy-tale setting by masses of silver-trimmed white and turquoise flowers. The music, exquisitely sung, lifted her spirits until Amy might have been floating.

Familiar faces smiled at her from the pews. As Amy paced down the aisle, she picked out Quent immediately. He sat to one side next to a likable, peppery hospital board member named Noreen McLanahan.

A shaft of sunshine through a side window bathed his strong face, which came alive as his eyes met hers. Amy felt his gaze travel down her body, awakening a swelling sensitivity in her breasts. She remembered her fantasy of walking down the aisle toward him in her own wedding gown. If only it were true. If only tonight were their wedding night...

He bowed his head to listen to a remark from his elderly companion, and the contact was broken. At the front of the church, Amy took her place beside Heather.

The organist segued into the bridal march. On her mother's arm, Natalie stepped into view.

The bride glided majestically between the rows of well-wishers, her attention fixed on the man who waited for her. There really was something magical about a wedding, Amy thought, watching joy radiate between the husband- and wife-to-be.

They were perfect for each other. With all her heart, she hoped that someday she might know that same happiness, that sense of coming home.

It was later in the service, when the choir began to sing "Climb Every Mountain," that she lost the battle with her tears. Amy let them flow. There was no reason to be embarrassed when half the congregation was weeping, too.

The vows were said and the rings exchanged. The couple turned to face their guests.

"May I present to you Dr. and Mrs. Patrick Barr!" said the pastor. Applause erupted from the onlookers.

Quent was clapping with the best of them. Beside him, Mrs. McLanahan jumped to her feet—not achieving much increase in stature, since she was so short— and topped the noise with a wolf whistle.

Patrick and Natalie burst out laughing. With a wave to the elderly woman, they strode up the aisle and out of sight.

As at the rehearsal, Amy was paired with Kent Lincoln, Mike's younger son. The six-year-old performed his task of groomsman solemnly, marching beside her with considerably more decorum than his eight-year-old brother who, ahead of them, tugged Heather into a near-lope.

Outside, limousines carried the bridal party to the Barr mansion a few blocks away. As they traced the curving driveway, Amy saw that the trees had been strung with Christmas lights, not yet aglow this early in the day. The front of the mansion, including the rounded roof of the portico, was hung with green wreaths and red and silver bows.

Christmas was still three weeks away. Amy didn't mind starting the celebration early, though. In fact, she loved it.

Once the limo halted in front of the house, they emerged into brisk afternoon sunshine. Inside, an enormous Christmas tree dominated the huge entryway with white lights, glass ornaments and—the bridesmaids began chuckling—silken bunnies hanging among the branches.

"Those weren't here last year!" Heather exclaimed. "Natalie's adding her touch, and I like it."

Ribbons, bows, draped fabric and ornaments gave the rest of the large entrance chamber and the grand staircase a sumptuous air. Through double doors, Amy saw champagne flowing from a fountain in the living room. Waiters circulated with hors d'oeuvres and champagne flutes as workers set up a buffet table.

Across the room, Natalie clapped her hands for attention. "Okay, guys, let's form a receiving line!"

They barely had time to queue up before the guests began arriving. A short time later, Quent helped Noreen McLanahan inside and stood beside her, waiting to shake hands.

Usually, Noreen had enough pep to volunteer at the hospital gift shop in addition to being a donor and board member, but obviously she wasn't up to par today. Amy was pleased that Quent had taken the older woman under his wing.

When they reached her, he shook Amy's hand firmly and held it longer than necessary. "I'm glad we were able to get you to the church on time. You added a lot to the ceremony."

"Me?" Amy shook her head. "Bridesmaids are just set decoration for the bride."

"I'd like to see a few more brides around here," said Noreen. "Even on my not-so-good days, you can't keep me home when there's a wedding."

"We've been joking about who's going to catch the bridal bouquet," Amy told her. "No one's taking any bets."

She noticed that Quent's mouth was ajar. Surely he didn't think she was dropping a hint! That would be ridiculous, considering how he'd beaten a retreat when they started to get close. To forestall a possible awkward moment, she turned and introduced Noreen to Alana.

"You're as pretty as your sister," Noreen told her. "But I see you're already wearing a ring. I guess I can't get you married off."

"You're way too late for that," Alana agreed.

Other guests required Amy's attention. By the time she found a free moment, Quent and Noreen had disappeared.

More and more people arrived, including some city officials. Since they were customarily invited to Patrick's Christmas open house, they had been included today as well.

Heather stretched up and whispered in Amy's ear, "Guess who just got here?"

She checked the end of the line, which was growing shorter. "If it isn't our favorite chief of police!"

There'd been speculation as to whether Finn Sorrell would show up this year. For one thing, he was the brother of Spencer Sorrell, the doctor who'd retired suddenly after trying to make trouble for Patrick.

In addition, Finn was known for having given Natalie's family a hard time whenever he came across them. Although they were good people, they'd had a few minor run-ins with the law, which had been enough to make Finn and Spencer both look down their noses at Natalie and her mother.

However, the Barr open house was a highlight of the season in Serene Beach. The mayor and the school board president, among others, were sure to be here, and the police chief knew that if he didn't show up, others would assume he hadn't been invited.

His high forehead shining beneath the bright lights, Finn stood with his wife on his arm, waiting his turn to shake hands. "I wouldn't miss this for the world," Heather said. "I'm not sure whether I'd rather see him force himself to be nice to Natalie and Angie, or see Patrick throw him bodily out the door."

"My, aren't you in a feisty mood!" Amy said.

"I can't stand people who pick on anyone who's at a disadvantage, the way Finn and Sorrell used to bully Natalie," Heather responded. "I know what it's like to be the person that people point to as a bad example."

It was hard to picture Heather in that situation, now that she was a successful obstetrician, but Amy knew the Moms in Training complained of suffering such insults. "Old wounds take a long time to heal, don't they?"

"You've got that right!"

Finn and his wife passed down the line, stiff smiles pasted to their mouths. Amy and Heather couldn't resist peering around to watch them tender their best wishes to the bride and her mother.

The police chief made a slight bow and introduced his wife. She hovered nervously as if unsure whether to curtsey.

"Everything went smoothly," Amy murmured, relieved. "I'm glad to see the chief finally learned some manners."

"There's nothing like a generous helping of humble pie," Heather said. "Maybe he'll be more careful who he picks on in the future."

Bernie, who always co-hosted the Barr open house, came to tell the bridesmaids they were free to go eat now. From her broad grin, anyone could see she was delighted about her brother's marriage.

Amy wandered through the mansion, enjoying the sumptuous decorations and the high spirits of the party-goers. Beautiful as this place was, though, she knew that if she were lucky enough to marry Quent, she wouldn't care where they lived.

When she spotted him standing near the terrace doors in the living room, enjoying the sunlit view of the harbor, Amy's throat tightened. She loved the strength of his jawline and the rebellious tuft of blond hair working its way upright at the crown of his head.

Well, she'd better not stand here with her heart in her eyes. There was enough gossip already going around Doctors Circle, and no doubt there'd be even more after their kissing scene in front of the church.

She filled a plate at the buffet. When she reached the dessert table, Quent materialized beside her, having already managed to snag his own food.

"I hear a rumor that there are vacant seats in the den," he told her. "Care to sit down?"

"Are you kidding?" Amy said. "My feet are killing me." Even the best-fitting high-heeled sandals began to hurt after a while.

Quent accompanied her into the oversize den, where a second Christmas tree sparkled in one corner. On the couch, Noreen held court between Dr. Dudley Fingger and Endowment Fund donor Alfred LoBianco. Both men were laughing at her witticisms.

"Isn't she amazing?" Quent held a chair for Amy, then perched on a folding chair beside her.

"I hope I'm that sharp when I reach her age," she said.

"I wish I were that sharp now!" The two of them shared a smile.

A rush of happiness swept over Amy. She felt utterly contented right this minute, being here with Quent. She didn't want to think about the future or the past, about where this might lead or whether she'd be a fraud if she caught Natalie's bouquet. She just wanted to stay next to Quent.

So, naturally, his cell phone rang. It was an occupational hazard of being a doctor, she reflected ruefully as he answered.

"Dr. Ladd." His easygoing expression vanished. "Slow down, Greg. What's going on?"

Greg, Amy remembered, was his nephew. How old had he said the boy was? She had the impression he was awfully young to be telephoning his uncle.

A moment later, Quent said, "I'll be there as soon as I can. You know it takes an hour and a half, but I'll step on it. Greg, you have to act like a grown-up until I get there or until Lucy or your baby-sitter comes back. Try to make your sister laugh so she'll stop crying, okay? I'm sure your aunt will be there any minute. I'm on my way." After a few more reassurances, he rang off.

"What's wrong?" Amy asked.

"I'm sorry, but I have to go." He set his plate on an end table. "Greg's aunt went running and left the kids with a teenage neighbor named Jenny. For some reason, she's gone outside and they're alone. Thank goodness Greg remembered how to speed-dial my number.''

He was already on his feet. Amy rose, too. "Should you call the police?''

"I hate to do that. It'll get Lucy in trouble and this isn't exactly her fault.'' Quent clenched his teeth, obviously torn. "But if they're in danger, I should, shouldn't I?''

"You could call back in five minutes and see if they're still alone,'' Amy said.

He nodded, relieved. "That's a good idea. Meanwhile, I've got to hit the road. I can't afford to wait.''

"I'm coming, too.'' She spoke without thinking, and more loudly than she'd intended. Suddenly she realized everyone in the room was watching.

When Quent hesitated, Amy's heart sank. She'd overstepped the bounds and made a fool of herself.

Worse than that, Quent was going to keep her out of what was obviously an important part of his life. She didn't intend to let him.

Chapter Ten

He had no right to drag Amy away from the wedding celebration, especially since she was one of the bridesmaids, Quent thought. Whatever happened to his niece and nephew, it wasn't her problem.

But he preferred not to be separated from her today. Their kiss had resounded through his entire being, reminding him that his feelings on Saturday night hadn't been an aberration at all.

He might not be ready to take on a serious relationship. He certainly didn't want to lure her from her busy, fulfilling life into a relationship that might deteriorate into misunderstandings and resentments, as had happened with his parents and, he gathered, with hers as well.

That didn't mean he had to give up her company. Being around her centered him and gave him strength. Besides, it might be useful to have a trained counselor on hand if matters got touchy in San Diego.

After hesitating longer than he'd intended, Quent decided to accept her offer. "Thanks," he said. "Let's go take our leave of Natalie and Patrick."

"I'll tell them," Noreen volunteered. "I heard

enough to know it's an emergency. They'll understand.''

"You're a sweetheart," Amy said.

"Hold on." Dr. Fingger was wearing his I'm-in-charge-here scowl. "Aren't you on call?"

"Nope," Quent said. He'd double-checked the bulletin board the day before.

"Are you sure?"

"Oh, for heaven's sake!" Noreen burst out. "If he is, I volunteer you to cover for him, Dudley."

"That hadn't occurred to me," Dr. Fingger said. "All right, Quent. I'll check with the hospital. If it turns out you're mistaken, I'll have the calls forwarded to me."

"I appreciate it." After they left the room, Quent said, "If I were on call, I'd know it. I don't take things like that lightly."

"I doubt Dr. Fingger meant to insult you," Amy said. "He strikes me as a person who has trouble trusting anyone but himself."

"Well, it was nice of him to offer to cover for me, even though he won't have to," Quent said. "And even though Noreen badgered him into it."

"She's good at that." Amy shot him a grin. "She nudges people to do what's right, and she usually gets her way."

They hurried through the crowd, out the front door and down the driveway to where Quent had left his SUV. He'd been lucky to find a space in Patrick's private parking area. Most of the guests had had to leave their cars across the street at Doctors Circle.

Before hitting the road, Quent dialed Lucy's number. To his relief, a young woman answered with a tentative, "Hello?"

"Is this Jenny?" Eager as he was to get moving, he preferred not to talk on the phone while driving.

"Uh, yes."

"This is the children's uncle, Dr. Ladd." He used his title when he wanted to impress people or intimidate them, as he did now. "My nephew called and said you left them alone."

"I forgot to take out my mom's trash like she told me and I knew she'd get mad, so I ran out for a minute." She sounded defensive. "I just live downstairs."

"It was long enough for Tara to get scared and start crying." Quent fought to keep his tone level, although his temper was rising.

"I saw my best friend outside and she had this big problem with her boyfriend and needed my advice. The kids were okay. I left them watching TV," Jenny said.

"Do you have any idea what can happen to a small child in a minute or two?" Briefly, he outlined some of the near-tragedies he'd seen as a doctor. "You will not let them out of your sight until Lucy gets back, is that understood?"

"Okay. I'm sorry," the girl said. Apparently he'd finally gotten through to her.

"I'm on my way there now." Quent put the car into gear. "If I find the children unattended, I'll have to call the police."

"Yes, sir. I mean, no, sir, they won't be alone."

"I'll see you soon." He didn't want her to know how long it would take, or she might duck out again.

"I'm glad she came back," Amy said after he hung up.

"Yes, but this situation can't go on," Quent said. "Although Lucy's done her best, I'm afraid she bit off more than she can chew. This baby-sitter is obviously

unqualified.'' He whipped onto St. Michel Drive, then
drove as fast as the speed limit allowed up Serene Boulevard toward the freeway.

''When you said the children lived with their aunt, I
pictured someone older,'' Amy said. ''I gather that's
not the case.''

''She's twenty-six.'' Calmer now, Quent told her
about the accident and how Lucy had been the only
family member to volunteer a home. ''It must have been
hard, even with a day-care center at work, to raise a
baby and a toddler. She's a kindhearted person and I
know she loves them, but she wasn't prepared.''

''Apparently she loves running on the weekends,''
Amy said. ''How did she manage until now?''

''She gave up running for a while,'' Quent said. ''A
few months ago, she told me she couldn't stand it any
more. She should have found a good sitter first.''

''She still might. This may be a transition period until
she lands the right person.''

Quent shook his head. ''Already there've been two
worrisome incidents. If Lucy isn't willing to give up
running...'' He let the words trail off as he reached the
freeway and hit the gas.

''What are the options?'' Amy asked. ''It might be
wise to prepare some suggestions before we get there.''

''You're right. I'll think about it.'' He appreciated
her logical approach. Although Quent had nerves of
steel when it came to emergencies at work, it was different when the situation involved people he loved.

''While you're thinking, I'm going to take a nap.''
Amy settled back, couldn't get comfortable in her hat,
and finally tossed it into the back seat.

Unrestrained, dark hair spilled across her shoulders,

while the turquoise dress brought out the freshness of her skin. What a lovely face she had, Quent mused.

At church, she'd been far and away the most beautiful woman walking down the aisle, not that he'd expected anyone else to recognize that fact when there was a bride to admire. In a way, he'd cherished being the one who appreciated her most.

The sexy, womanly sway to her movements had made him want to carry her off to a private place where they could resume their embrace. But it was best if they didn't. How long could magic last? he wondered. Perhaps forever, if you never forced it down to earth.

To help him concentrate on the road, Quent tuned the radio to a country station they both liked, then settled into a rhythm of driving. The freeway stretched for miles through the Orange County landscape with its gently rolling hills, shopping centers and fanned-out housing developments.

Soon they were passing the exits to San Juan Capistrano and San Clemente. As they left the thickest traffic behind and entered San Diego County, Quent allowed himself to acknowledge the idea that had been tickling the back of his mind.

He wanted to take charge of Tara and Greg. A year ago, as a neonatology resident sharing an apartment with two other men, he hadn't even considered it. Also, for months after the tragedy, he'd buried himself in work. It had been his way of keeping the universe from spinning out of control.

Now he had a steady job and had grown much stronger emotionally. More than that, he'd come to love Tara and Greg. Their personalities and their development fascinated him.

They'd popped into his mind frequently this week.

He'd stopped at a toy store and bought several gifts, which were tucked beneath the back seat of his SUV. He'd caught himself noticing the layout of playgrounds at nearby parks and had clipped a newspaper article about the best schools in the area.

He wanted to give the children a home where they would be safe. He wanted to guide them through childhood and adolescence, to provide the stability and the love that they deserved.

Of course, he didn't mean to fight Lucy for custody. He had to give her a chance to keep the children if she were willing to make changes. If not, he hoped she'd listen to reason.

Having chosen a course of action, Quent turned his attention to practical matters. "Do you know anything about day care in our area?" he asked.

Amy's eyelids fluttered open. "My aunt runs a licensed home center."

"What about preschools?" he asked.

"My aunt's mentioned a good one near her," she said. "She drives one of her kids there and back in the mornings. Why?"

"Because I intend to take Greg and Tara, if Lucy will let me."

His words hung in the air for several seconds. "That's quite a decision," Amy said. "Are you sure you've considered all the angles?"

"Are you implying that I'm impulsive?" Quent replied, half teasing.

"Impulsive? Well, let's see." Amy assumed a mock-serious attitude. "There was the time you came to work dressed as a pirate and announced that you planned to wear costumes to the clinic until Halloween. Which, as I recall, was three weeks off."

"That was a bit over the top, I admit." Quent had done it mostly to annoy his former supervisor, Dr. Sorrell. He'd succeeded.

"Then there's the Ping-Pong table in your living room," she said.

"What could be more practical than having recreational facilities right in my own home?" Quent joked.

"How old are these children again? I forget," Amy said.

"Greg's four. Tara's fifteen—no, sixteen months now," he said.

"They won't even be able to reach the Ping-Pong table," she pointed out.

"They can stand on stepstools. Or I'll get rid of it."

They passed through the open expanse of Camp Pendleton, with the Pacific Ocean shining to their right. At last, Amy said, "You're serious about this?"

"Yes." An alarm sounded in Quent's mind at the immense task he'd be taking on, but he reminded himself of how much the kids needed him.

He would always fear the nearness of an abyss, the one he'd sensed the other night when Amy nearly fell into the harbor. Certainly he would never forget the shock of losing his mother, brother and sister-in-law. He had to protect the children, no matter what it cost him.

For all his playful self-indulgences, Quent recognized that the time had come to put others' needs first. In a sense, he'd been preparing for this for a long time. The desire to make his life count for something, to be of use, had inspired him to go to medical school, and it came to the fore now.

"I'm afraid I won't be free to play video games and

hang out as much as I used to," he said. "I hope you won't take this personally."

"Personally?" Amy glowered at him. "Quentin Ladd, do you think I'm going to be offended because you want to take in two orphaned children?"

"When you put it that way, I guess not." Her indignation gave him new hope. "We can all schedule play dates together."

"Play dates?" Amy glared even harder. "Someone will have to watch them when you're working evenings or weekends. Not that I have much experience with children, but I can do that."

He wanted to hug her and hold her close. Quent had never expected this much generosity, not even from his best friend. "I'll take all the help I can get," he said. "You'd be a lifesaver."

"It's essential for a parent to have a backup," Amy said. "That's what Lucy lacks."

"That, and an understanding of the children's long-term needs." He recalled Lucy's casual attitude about preschool.

"Do you?" Amy challenged.

"I'll get one."

The more he thought about it, the more excited he grew. Quent knew parenthood could be exhausting, but it was challenging and miraculous, too.

With Amy at his side, they'd not only manage, they would triumph. His imagination leaped ahead to picnics on the beach and trips to Disneyland. Well, maybe he'd hold off on the amusement park until the kids got older, but there were lots of other fun things to do.

And they'd mean a whole lot more with Amy around.

He'd learn to cook nutritious food. Stock up on children's books. Hide the TV remote control so they could only watch educational shows. Of course, that meant he couldn't watch kung-fu movies except late at night, but he'd manage.

There might be a hitch or two along the way. It was nothing he couldn't overcome with his best friend's help.

AMY HOPED Quent wasn't making a mistake. The last thing two orphaned children needed was to be bounced from one home to another and then not have it work out.

She knew he'd do his best. But she doubted a bachelor like him had any idea of what lay ahead.

Even Amy, despite her training in family counseling, lacked practical experience. She was game to learn, though. With Heather becoming a mother and a grandmother at the same time, Amy knew who to go to for advice on diaper-changing and baby-sitting.

There was another point she couldn't ignore. Sharing the children should bring Quent and her closer. It might help him get past whatever emotional block was holding him back.

Still, she hadn't offered her help with any ulterior motive. She intended to fulfill her promise regardless of whether matters between them remained at the casual level.

Amy studied Quent's profile, silhouetted against the late-afternoon sunlight. There was a new maturity in the way he held himself, she thought, as if the prospect of fatherhood was already toning down his wilder side.

She vowed silently to do her best to make sure

this new arrangement, if Lucy agreed to it, worked out happily for everyone.

"I'M SORRY, but I can't let you have them," Lucy told Quent.

They were sitting in her kitchen, drinking herbal tea. Amy sat at one end of the table, listening without saying much.

By the time Quent and Amy had arrived twenty minutes earlier, Lucy had returned and Jenny was long gone. The children, after joyfully greeting their uncle, had retreated to their shared bedroom with their new toys.

According to Lucy, the sitter had given a version of events in which she merely poked her head out the door for a minute. Even when Quent explained that Jenny had earlier admitted going outside and chatting with a girlfriend, all Lucy had said was, "No harm done. I know the girl means well."

As diplomatically as possible, Quent had proposed that the children come to live with him. He could swear he'd seen relief flash across Lucy's face, yet, maddeningly, she was refusing.

"I know you love them," he said. "And no one admires what you've done more than I do. But it's obviously hard on you. And I'd really like to have them."

"There's no point in talking about it." Lucy folded her hands in front of her. "Things are fine the way they are."

"Do you plan to continue running on Saturdays? You can't keep using pickup sitters." Quent struggled to use a nonjudgmental tone. The last thing he intended was to offend her. "Look at the problems that you…that we've had recently."

"Jenny's eager to do it and she's learning. She won't leave them again." Lucy's tone verged on snappish.

"There's no reason for you to march in here and try to take over."

Quent was about to argue when he caught a warning glance from Amy. Family counseling was her territory, so he held back.

"May I ask you something?" Amy said to Lucy.

"Sure, I guess."

"I get the impression you're holding something back, perhaps out of politeness. That there's an additional reason why you don't feel right about accepting Quent's offer," she said. "It might clear the air if you could tell him what it is."

"You're pretty sharp," Lucy said. "That's true, but…" She stopped.

"Go on," Amy said.

"He might get mad."

"If you're going to say I haven't contributed as much as you think I should, that's okay," Quent said. "I admit I could have done more."

"That's not it." Lucy drummed her fingers on the scarred surface of the table. "It's something my sister said."

"Paula?" Quent didn't know the two women had ever discussed him. "What did she tell you?"

"Nothing bad. I mean, it was personal." Lucy cleared her throat. "This is kind of embarrassing."

"Would you prefer if he left the room and you told it to me?" Amy said.

Lucy considered, then shook her head. "No, it's okay. See, a few years ago, I had kind of a crush on Quent."

"You did?" He'd never had a clue about it. Before the tragedy, he had only a vague recollection of meeting

Lucy at his brother's wedding and on a few family occasions.

"Sure, the handsome doctor and all that." Lucy waved one hand, dismissing her girlish fantasies. "Then Paula gave me a talking-to. She said you were a playboy, not the kind of a man I could rely on."

"At the time, she was right," Quent conceded. "I put all my energy into my studies. When it came to my private life, I just looked for a party."

"I'm not sure Paula would have liked her children to be raised by a single father," Lucy explained. "And I'm sure she wouldn't have approved of you. Even though recently you seem to have changed."

From her words, Quent sensed that, underneath, Lucy wanted him to convince her. She'd already admitted that he'd changed. Now he had to give her a good reason to believe her sister would have chosen him to raise Greg and Tara.

He had to do it now. This window of opportunity, of sharing confidences, was going to close. If he couldn't persuade Lucy to trust him today, her resolve might harden and he would never succeed.

All of a sudden, he knew how to convince her. He had to do it for the children's sakes, even though it was a risk. *Act now, deal with the consequences later.* That was another of Quent's mottos.

"I suppose Amy and I shouldn't keep you in the dark any longer," he said. "We want you to be the first to know. We're getting married."

There was a moment's silence. At the end of the table, Amy sat frozen with her tea mug in one hand.

"Really? That's fantastic!" Lucy's face brightened. "If you're going to be married, that's another story entirely."

Quent tried to catch Amy's eye to send her a visual plea for cooperation. It would be too bad if honesty forced her to contradict what he'd said.

They'd be raising the children together, as they'd already agreed. Maybe they could even share quarters, since it would be more practical for her to watch the children that way.

As soon as the possibility entered his mind, he seized on it. What could be better than moving in with his best friend? It would be good for him and good for the youngsters.

Amy could still lead her independent life. He wouldn't have to worry about them storing up resentments or having to confront heavy issues. They'd be friends, the way they were now.

"So when's the big day?" Lucy asked.

Since Amy apparently wasn't going to answer, Quent improvised. "We haven't set one. We haven't even formally announced our engagement. That's why Amy's not wearing a ring. But I could see that you needed to know, so you can understand that I've matured. I think Paula would approve, don't you?"

"I'm sure she would," Lucy said. "Wow. Congratulations, Amy."

"Thank you," Amy said distractedly.

It was as good as an acknowledgement. Quent owed her a big debt for this one.

Thank goodness people often had long engagements. Eventually, he supposed, they'd have to officially break it off, but by then he should be able to impress Lucy with what a terrific job he was doing.

"It'll take me a few days to sort through things and pack their stuff. I'm going to miss them, but I'll admit, I've been worried about how I was going to meet their

needs in the future." Despite a trace of regret, Lucy
sounded cheerful. "You can pick them up in a few
days. Would Wednesday evening be all right?"

"Absolutely."

They adjourned to tell the children the news. Beam-
ing, Greg threw his arms around his uncle. Tara, who
was too young to understand, went to sit on Amy's lap
and tried on her bridesmaid's hat. Fitting low over her
forehead, it hung at a funny angle.

"She's a sweetheart." Amy hugged the little girl.
"My goodness, we'll have to buy you a hat of your
own."

"If you don't mind my asking, how come you're so
dressed up?" Lucy said.

"We were at my best friend's wedding reception."
When Tara slipped off her lap, Amy got down on the
floor to play with her.

"You were a bridesmaid?" Lucy said. "And you let
Quent drag you away to see two children you'd never
met? You must really love this guy."

"You bet." Keeping her face averted, Amy nudged
a block into place so it didn't fall off the tower Tara
was building. "She has good hand-eye coordination for
her age."

"You know a lot about kids."

"In the theoretical sense. I'm a family counselor,"
Amy explained.

"Perfect!" Lucy appeared to be releasing her last
reservation. "Quent, I'm glad this worked out. It's going to be tough giving them up, but I think Paula would
prefer them to be in a two-parent home."

"You've done a great job," he told her. "More than
anyone had a right to ask."

"Thanks. It got pretty overwhelming sometimes."

Quent and Amy stayed awhile longer, playing with the children. By the time they left, Lucy was hugging the kids tightly, but she hadn't changed her mind.

They'd done the right thing, he reflected, for everyone involved. Except maybe for Amy.

He hoped she could find it in her heart to forgive him.

Chapter Eleven

Amy barely held herself in check while Quent negotiated side streets in the early darkness. Although she wasn't exactly angry, she couldn't believe he'd conned her into a phony engagement.

She hated to lie. If she'd exposed him, however, it would have killed any chance he had of winning Lucy's consent.

As soon as they hit the freeway and he didn't have to concentrate so hard on his driving, she blurted, "I knew you were impulsive, but not *this* impulsive!"

He gave her a rueful grin. "I even managed to catch myself off guard."

"As your alleged wife-to-be, I hope you'll refrain from making any more commitments without consulting me. What do you plan to do next, volunteer me to run for the school board?" She hadn't realized how steamed she was until the words spilled out.

"Calm down," Quent said. "I know I was out of line. Don't you ever get a gut instinct that you have to act now or you'll never get a second chance?"

Amy didn't want to encourage the man's cheekiness, but she understood what he meant. "I suppose so, but I don't like deceiving Lucy."

"I apologize," Quent said. "I would have discussed it with you first but I had no idea Paula had told her I was a playboy."

"Well, what's done is done," Amy said. "Where do we go from here?"

"Good question." His expression sober, Quent switched lanes and accelerated up a long grade. "I didn't have time to consider anything past Wednesday night. If you want nothing to do with this whole situation, I won't hold it against you."

"What about the kids?" she said.

He released a long breath. "That's the problem. The more I think about it, the more I realize I can't raise them without you. What do you think of them?"

"They're darling." Amy retained a sensory impression of Tara sitting on her lap trying to fit together two pieces of a preschool puzzle, her small face scrunched in concentration, her hair smelling of baby shampoo. Before tonight, Amy had ached for a child. Now she wanted *these* children. "Raising them is a long-term commitment, you know."

"I can't plan too far ahead at this point," Quent admitted. "If we're agreed in principle that we're going to raise them together, let's take it one step at a time."

Amy had to make a decision. Common sense warred with her heart, and her heart won. "I'll do it."

He gave her a look of sheer gratitude. "You'll never regret it."

"Let's hope not," she said.

He reached out and cupped one hand around her chin. "Thank you."

The gesture dispelled any lingering doubts. It connected them in such a gentle, intimate way that Amy knew she belonged with Quent, as his friend or fiancée or whatever else he needed.

He returned both hands to the wheel. "I'm sorry my late sister-in-law saw me as a playboy, but I've matured a lot since then. I intend to be the best dad ever."

"Lying to Lucy hardly proves your maturity," Amy pointed out. "How long do you think it will take her to get suspicious?"

"There's no reason for her to, if we make the right arrangements." He glanced at her uncertainly. "Amy, I know I've asked a lot of you today, but I have one more request, and it's a big one."

"Since there's evidently no limit to your chutzpah, go ahead and ask."

"My one-room apartment isn't suitable for raising a family. I can find a bigger one, but it will take time," Quent said. "May the kids and I stay at your condo? I'll pay my share of the mortgage and utilities, of course. In fact, I'll pay extra."

There was no sense in reviewing all the good reasons for refusing. Amy knew she was going to give in, so why fight it?

That didn't mean he got his way about everything. "I'm not doing your laundry," she said.

"I don't expect it. I'll handle mine and the kids'." After a moment, Quent added, "I'll cook, too."

"How are you at taking out garbage?"

"Masterful."

"That's promising," Amy said. "Right now, your biggest job will be childproofing. I can't even move in until Wednesday evening myself because of the repair work."

"I'll stock up on cabinet locks and outlet guards,"

Quent said. "And I'll pick up car seats for both of our vehicles. Is there a lock on your pool gate?"

"Yes, and the tenants are good about keeping it shut." Amy's mind raced ahead. "Tara will need a crib. What about a bed for Greg?"

"Lucy might let us take the children's furniture." For the next few miles, they discussed practical matters.

Amy was trying to figure out a diplomatic way to broach the subject of sleeping arrangements when Quent brought it up himself. "I'm assuming we'll have separate bedrooms."

"I suppose so," she said.

"We're doing this for the kids," Quent said. "That's the most important thing."

He was right, Amy supposed. They needed to take this one step at a time, not complicate matters by rushing into intimacy. "Of course."

"You know, I love them," he said.

Amy nearly stopped breathing until she heard the word "them." For the span of a few words, she'd thought he was going to say he loved *her*. "I never saw you as the daddy type before," she managed to reply.

"Neither did I," Quent said. "People change."

"Yes, they do."

A few weeks ago, through the window of the Birthing Center nursery, Amy had watched Quent examine a baby with tender thoroughness. But there'd been something different about him today as he played with his niece and nephew, a fiercely protective air that she hadn't seen before.

Amy suspected he was going to change even more in the weeks to come. She wondered if he would ever reach the point of wanting to be a husband as well as a father.

When that happened, she hoped he'd discover deeper, more romantic feelings toward her. That she'd be the one he fell in love with, and not remain the old friend with whom he shared good times until he was ready to give his heart to someone else.

AT LUNCHTIME on Monday, Heather dropped into Amy's office. "Did you get the word about who caught Natalie's bouquet?"

"I haven't heard a peep." Absorbed in preparing for the children's arrival, she'd forgotten the matter entirely. "Who's the lucky girl?"

"You are."

"The paint fumes must be affecting me." Although she'd hardly noticed the lingering smell until now, Amy went over and opened a window. "I could have sworn you said I caught the bouquet."

"You did. By proxy."

This was a new twist. "I didn't know you could catch a bridal bouquet by proxy," she said.

"According to Noreen McLanahan, you can." Heather gave her red hair a shake of disbelief. "Frankly, I didn't buy it, but Natalie gave her permission."

"Noreen stood in as my proxy?" Amy didn't know whether to laugh or bristle.

"I wouldn't have believed that little old lady could leap so high. She puts the Lakers in the shade," Heather said.

"She could hardly walk up the steps on Saturday!"

"She claimed her medication kicked in," the obstetrician said. "I'd like to try some of that medicine myself. Want to go eat in the courtyard?"

"Sure." Amy grabbed her brown bag from a desk drawer and accompanied her friend outside.

Red and green poinsettias spilled from the terra-cotta pots that flanked the fountain. Most of the small, round tables were filled, but the two women claimed a newly vacated one. Despite the cool December air, the southern California sunshine warmed Amy's shoulders.

As she set out her cream-cheese-and-cucumber sandwich, Amy said, "Noreen wasn't far off course. I got engaged on Saturday."

Heather paused with a carrot stick halfway to her mouth. "Excuse me?"

"Quent popped the question. Unfortunately, he didn't pop it to me." She enjoyed her friend's mystified reaction. Such a strange story was best told in an offbeat manner.

"You're going to have to start from the beginning," Heather said.

"He asked his late sister-in-law's sister to give him custody of his niece and nephew," Amy said. "She wasn't impressed with the idea of a bachelor father, so he volunteered me as his fiancée."

"Without asking you first?" Heather resumed munching, her attention fixed on Amy.

"It happened spontaneously."

"Things usually do with Quent, or so I gather," said her friend. "Don't tell me you're going along with this!"

"Call me a sucker, but those kids are adorable," Amy said. "He and they are moving into my condo on Wednesday. It's strictly platonic. I don't want to lie to other people. If I show up wearing a ring, I guess we will just let them draw their own conclusions."

"I wish Natalie were here. She'd get a kick out of

this,'' Heather said. "On the other hand, I'm sure she prefers being on her honeymoon."

"Soft Caribbean breezes." Amy sighed.

"A hard, willing husband." Heather chuckled.

"That's downright cruel, considering Quent and I are sleeping in different bedrooms," Amy told her.

"Does he know you're a virgin?" Heather kept her voice low.

"What do you want to do, ruin my reputation?" Amy teased.

"Don't be too eager to give it up," Heather warned. "Unless a guy loves you whole-heartedly, it's best to keep him at bay. Take it from a woman who's been there."

"Did you ever think maybe it was time you took another chance?" She avoided making a direct reference to Olive's no-account father. The subject was still a sore point, she knew.

"I haven't met the right guy." Heather's mouth tightened. "Not that I want to."

"Why do I get the impression there's something you're not telling me?"

"A little over a year ago, I nearly made a big mistake with a guy. Thank goodness circumstances intervened." Heather wrinkled her nose, looking more like a teenager than a grandmother. "I have no desire to put my heart through the wringer again. Still, weren't Natalie and Patrick radiant?"

For the rest of their lunch break, they reminisced about the wedding, rejoicing in their friends' happiness. At one o'clock, Amy returned to her office for an appointment with Cynthia Hernandez.

The young nurse had more bad news about her boyfriend. He and his wife were moving to Alaska. And he'd revealed that he already had three kids.

"I made him show me their pictures to prove he wasn't lying," Cynthia said. "I don't believe anything he says anymore."

She still wanted to keep the twins, even though she intended to have no further contact with the man. Fortunately, the pregnancy was going well.

The session ended on a positive note. Still, Amy knew there was no easy resolution to Cynthia's predicament.

After the young woman left, Amy was making notes in her computer when a knot of silver-trimmed turquoise and white flowers dropped onto her desk. She looked up to see Mrs. McLanahan regarding her sternly.

"I kept this in the refrigerator all weekend," said the older woman, who wore the striped uniform of a gift shop volunteer. "You are to take it home and treat it with reverence."

"It's beautiful." Amy put the bouquet to her nose and inhaled the fresh perfume. "Thank you."

Noreen tapped her desk. "I've always believed there's a magic to bouquets once they've been caught, but it doesn't last forever. I expect you to make good use of this opportunity, particularly as concerns a certain young doctor of our acquaintance."

Amy considered mentioning her pseudo-engagement but decided against it. Mrs. McLanahan would read far too much into the matter. "I've got a rope in my trunk," she joked. "Want to help me lasso him on his way out today?"

"Make sport of me all you want. I'll have the last laugh." The widow managed to keep a straight face, although Amy suspected she was kidding. "I'll be watching the mail for my wedding invitation."

"I promise, you'll be the first to know," she said.

Although still lovely, the flowers were drooping by the time Amy carried them home for the day. There was no sign of Quent as she walked by the Well-Baby Clinic and she decided not to stop in.

In only a few days, they'd be seeing plenty of each other. The thought of it made Amy nervous. What were they going to talk about at breakfast every day?

She supposed she was about to find out.

QUENT GRABBED the training cup halfway to the floor. "Good catch, eh?" he said, and checked for his nephew's reaction.

"She threw it on purpose," Greg said solemnly.

"No harm done." With a paper napkin, Quent wiped the spilled drops of milk as he replaced the cup on the high chair's tray. Although a few drops had landed on his bathrobe, he pretended not to notice.

"Are you sure she's too old for a bottle?" Amy asked, tightening her own robe. The white terry cloth tended to gap at the top, revealing her smooth throat and a hint of something lower down that Quent struggled to ignore.

"Bob-bob!" Tara bounced in her chair.

"That means bottle," Greg explained. "She wants her bottle."

"Bottles are bad for her teeth." Quent was determined to start off right when it came to health. "She's old enough to use a cup all the time now."

He'd collected the children last night. Amy had welcomed them to her remodeled condo, which she'd aired out to minimize the scents of new carpet and touched-up paint.

The children were fascinated by the video-game system, which she'd allowed Greg to play with supervision. He had tossed a few blunt-tipped darts, too, until Quent realized small pieces might come loose if Tara found one and chewed on it. The darts had been put away with the promise that they'd play another time while the little girl napped.

Since they'd shared a room at Lucy's apartment, the youngsters didn't mind doing so again. Quent and Amy had reassembled Tara's crib and Greg's youth bed, while, for himself, Quent had made up the pull-out couch in Amy's home office.

After a night on the thin mattress, his back felt stiff. He'd get the knots out when he found time to exercise, although, since he was working until seven tonight, that might not happen today.

Well, he'd expected to encounter a few kinks while settling in, although not in his sacroiliac. On the plus side, Aunt Mary had space for the two children in day care and, at her suggestion, Quent would sign Greg up for preschool right after New Year's.

"I like this cereal," the little boy said. "Is there more?"

"There should be. We just opened it." Amy peered into the box. "Where'd it all go?"

Guiltily, Quent glanced at his bowl. He and Greg had snacked on cereal last night and he'd eaten two helpings for breakfast. "Sorry."

"I guess a half-gallon of milk wasn't enough, either." Amy indicated the empty carton. "Can you stop by the supermarket later?"

"You mean tonight?" Quent's dismay must have

shown on his face. He knew it wasn't fair to burden Amy, who'd only volunteered to baby-sit now and then, but his workload today was a killer.

"Do you have to stay late?" she said.

He nodded. "I'll get take-out food on the way home, if you don't mind waiting until seven-thirty to eat." So much for his intention of cooking a healthy meal every night. "Do you suppose you could feed the kids?"

According to Lucy, Greg liked peanut-butter sandwiches as well as pasta, and Tara could eat baby food in a pinch. He'd posted a list of their preferences on the refrigerator.

"No problem," Amy said. "Eight o'clock's bedtime, so you can kiss them good-night and then we'll have dinner *à deux*."

"That would be great." Being around her gave Quent confidence in the future and a quiet sense of happiness. It was more than he'd expected.

Last night when it was time to put the children to bed, she'd cuddled Tara and crooned a lullaby. As Quent listened, the day's tensions had seeped away.

Her singing had reminded him of innocent times long ago, when the world felt safe. He wanted to float away on the sound of Amy's voice.

Although moving in together hadn't originally been part of his plan, Quent liked it better with every passing moment. He'd missed being part of a real home.

"I'll pick up the kids at Aunt Mary's and stop at the supermarket after work," Amy said.

"I don't want to take advantage of you," he protested. "I know you hate shopping for food."

She reached out to catch Tara's cup as, once again, it teetered near the edge of the tray. "With the kids along, it'll be an adventure."

"Thanks," he said. "We'll get a system worked out soon so we don't end up in crunches like this."

"I suspect crunches go with the territory." When Amy got up to clear the remains of breakfast, he hurried to help her.

Once they'd loaded the dishwasher, it was past time to get ready for work. Even with two bathrooms, they were in danger of running late.

While Greg watched TV in the living room, Quent and Amy agreed that Tara would be safe playing unsupervised in her room. A child gate blocked the doorway, and she had plenty of toys to keep her busy.

Quent was getting out of the shower when he heard Tara shriek. Grabbing a towel, he flung it around his waist and ran into the hall.

At the same time, Amy darted from her bedroom. Her hair tumbled from beneath a shower cap and the bathrobe clung to her damp skin.

"Did you hear that?" she gasped. "Tara! Are you all right?"

Whack! A toy flew over the childproof gate and crashed into the opposing wall. Another shriek followed. This time, Quent recognized it for what it was: laughter.

Coming abreast of the opening, he barely missed getting smacked by a cloth book. "Dada!" Tara greeted him, and held out her arms to be picked up.

"She called me Dada!" he said, elated. Every instinct urged him to whirl the little girl in the air, except for one obstacle: He'd have to let go of the towel first.

"Well? Are you just going to stand there?" Amy demanded with a grin. Obviously, she'd noticed his dilemma. "Come on, Daddy, you're not going to let a little false modesty get in the way of playing with your baby, are you?''

''*You* could take her.'' Playfully, he eyed the bathrobe she was holding shut. ''I promise I won't look. Well, maybe I'll peek, but I'll never tell anybody what I see.''

Her gaze scorching his body, she opened her mouth as if to make a retort. Nothing came out. Quent couldn't speak, either. Awareness swelled inside him of her velvety skin and his own bare torso. Of how tantalizing she would feel pressed to him, her breasts grazing his chest, her hands dropping the robe to stroke his hips. In the hallway, he heard his own ragged breathing, matched by hers.

A teddy bear whacked into his shoulder. ''Da!'' shouted Tara.

''Way to go!'' said Amy. ''Hit him again, kid!''

''Hey!'' Quent protested.

''Ten points if you make him drop the towel,'' she told Tara. ''We women have to stick together.''

''No fair ganging up.'' Quent returned to the bathroom with as much dignity as he could salvage. Which, in a towel, wasn't much.

Okay, so there were bound to be a few miscues on the road to perfect parenthood, he told himself as he dried off and got dressed. With luck, his physically excited state would subside by the time he dropped the children at day care.

He was definitely looking forward to that private dinner with Amy tonight.

Chapter Twelve

Letting Greg push a miniature cart provided by the supermarket had seemed like a good idea when Amy arrived at the store. She changed her mind the third time he raced out of sight down an adjoining aisle.

Why had she ever quibbled about shopping back in the days when all she had to do was stroll down the aisles at her own pace? That would be an unimaginable luxury for a woman with two tots.

By the time she reached Greg, he'd piled half a dozen items into his basket. ''Please put these back.'' Amy demonstrated by returning a box of crackers to the shelf. ''You can carry the cereal if you want to.''

Seated in Amy's cart, Tara clapped her hands with glee. ''Mick!'' she announced, and pointed to the milk carton beside her.

''That's right, it's milk,'' Amy said. Much as she wanted to encourage Tara's language acquisition, it was hard to concentrate with both children demanding her attention.

''I'll keep the cookies,'' Greg announced, snatching a package she'd been on the verge of removing.

''Okay, I suppose a little dessert won't hurt anything.'' Amy knew Quent planned to fix healthy food for the kids, but surely there was leeway for sweets. Keeping one eye on the kids, she finished restoring the other items he'd collected to their proper places.

"I'm hungry." The little boy pried at the cellophane wrapping. "I want to eat my snack now."

"It's almost dinnertime, honey." Amy groaned to hear herself sounding like a stereotypical mother. But what else could she say?

"Cookie!" Tara demanded and waggled her fingers at her brother.

"Later, guys." Amy lifted the package from Greg's grasp.

He stomped his foot and glared at her, a picture of four-year-old outrage. Reacting to his mood, Tara began to scream for a cookie.

Amy stared at them in dismay. She treasured these kids, and she knew that, underneath, they were fond of her. She didn't want to come across as some kind of ogre, but she counseled parents on dealing with exactly this kind of situation. "If you let them win by throwing temper tantrums, they're in control," was her standard line.

She hadn't realized how difficult it would be to stand tough, especially with other shoppers glaring as if she must have done something cruel to make the kids scream this way. "I'm sorry but the answer is still no," she told Greg. "You and Tara can eat cookies after supper. Let's go check out."

"I'm hungry!" he bellowed louder than she would have dreamed possible for such a small child.

"Cookie!" shrieked Tara.

Amy didn't notice who was pushing a cart toward her until she heard Mrs. McLanahan say, "What have we here? I know these aren't yours."

"It's a long story," Amy told her. "Let's just say that they're my responsibility."

Today, she'd told her secretary about letting Quent and the kids stay at her condo, which meant the story ought to be spreading far and wide. She wasn't looking forward to dealing with the inevitable questions and assumptions. In any case apparently word hadn't reached Mrs. McLanahan.

"Care for a suggestion?" the widow asked.

"I'd be grateful," she said.

"Open the package and give them each one cookie now. If they behave themselves, they can have more after dinner," Mrs. McLanahan advised.

"I always tell parents not to give in to tantrums," Amy said, torn between the desire to do what was right and the need to restore peace.

"When kids are overtired or hungry, they can't control themselves," the elderly woman told her. "Next time, give them a snack before you go grocery shopping."

"That's a good idea. Thank you." Amy opened the package and handed each child a cookie. "That's all you get until after dinner. If you fuss any more, I'll put them away till tomorrow."

"Okay." Greg wolfed his down. He looked ashamed of himself. "I'm sorry I fussed."

"You're forgiven."

Tara tore her cookie into two pieces, gobbled one and stuck the other up her nose. Amy, Noreen and Greg all started to laugh. Delighted to be the center of attention, the baby chortled and out flew the cookie fragment. Tara didn't seem to mind.

Mrs. McLanahan departed without inquiring further.

Judging by the twinkle in her eyes, however, she hadn't given up on hearing wedding bells.

The children were little angels on the trip home, and they ate their dinner messily but without protest. Afterward, Amy gave them each more cookies and helped get them ready for bed.

"Uncle Quent will be home soon," she told Greg. "You can stay up till he gets here."

He yawned. "Will you help me say my prayers?"

"Of course." Amy hoped Quent wouldn't mind if they went ahead. She could see that children operated on their own timetable.

The boy knelt by the bed and bowed his round head so all she could see was a tumble of brown hair. In Amy's arms, Tara curled sleepily.

"Dear God, thanks for the cookies," Greg said. "Please send more tomorrow. Amen."

"Is that the way Lucy taught you to say prayers?" Amy asked, trying to hide her amusement.

"No." Greg, who'd hopped to his feet, knelt again. "Dear God, it's me again. Thanks for Amy and Uncle Quent. Thanks for Aunt Lucy, too. I like our new home. Please let me use the dartboard again soon. Amen." He slanted an uncertain glance at her. "Is that okay?"

"It's fine," she said.

In the other room, the phone rang. Amy hurried to answer.

It was Lucy, anxious to confirm that the kids were doing well. Amy put them each on the phone in turn, although Tara wasn't capable of carrying on much of a conversation.

Afterwards, she spoke to Lucy again. "How are you doing? You must miss them a lot."

"I do," the other woman admitted. "There's an upside, though. At work today, we got really busy. It was a relief to be able to stay late without worrying about the hours at the day-care center. I'm sorry. That probably sounds hard-hearted.''

"Working mothers always feel torn between one obligation and another." It was an issue that came up frequently with Amy's clients.

"That's the truth," Lucy said. "Is Quent there?"

"He's not home yet. I'm expecting him any minute."

"He's lucky to have you." Lucy's sigh reverberated over the phone. "There's a lot to be said for the two-parent family."

"That's for sure. You deserve a medal for what you've done this past year," Amy said.

"I feel a bit guilty about relinquishing the children," Lucy admitted. "I keep telling myself it's for the best."

"I'm sure it is."

Fifteen minutes later, Quent arrived, tired but happy, surrounded by the scent of take-out fried chicken. "I've been thinking about you and the kids all day," he said as he handed over the sacks of food and pulled off his jacket. "This sure beats coming home to an empty apartment."

"For me, too." As Amy followed him into the children's room and watched him hug them, her heart swelled with longing.

She wanted this to be real. She wanted these to be her children, for Quent to be her husband. Then, after dinner, the two of them would go to bed together and hold each other all night.

Her body quickened. This morning, she'd itched to run her hands over his half-naked body and strip away the towel. He'd clearly responded to her, too.

In the past, each time they'd nearly made love, fate

had intervened. After she nearly fell into the harbor, Quent had abruptly withdrawn, and she still didn't understand why. Surely he would begin to change now that they were living together. Would tonight be a turning point? She wondered if she would finally find out how it felt to become his lover, and whether she dared to take that step, knowing that he didn't love her.

The children fell asleep as soon as their heads hit their pillows. The adults made a beeline for the kitchen.

Quent set out paper containers on the table. "I hope you like the meal."

"It's one of my favorites." The smell of chicken, corn bread and mashed potatoes went directly to Amy's stomach. She produced plates and cutlery, and the two of them dug in. "How was work today?"

"We had a preemie this morning, five weeks early. Healthy as a horse," he said.

"That must have been a relief."

"It sure was." He downed some food before adding, "The clinic was busy, as usual. Nothing out of the ordinary. The flu season appears to be mild this year."

"That's a blessing."

"I'd like to hear about your day, but I guess you can't talk about your clients, can you?"

She paused with a drumstick in one hand. "No. I can share Mrs. Ryerson's gossip, though. One of the admitting clerks got caught raising a lion at home."

"A full-size lion?" he asked in amazement.

"Can you believe that? She bought it as a cub and tried to keep it shut up in her home."

"And nobody noticed?"

"She told people she had a big dog." Amy shook her head in disbelief at the woman's nerve.

"What gave her away?"

"The neighbors finally figured out that the roaring wasn't coming from her stereo system."

He chuckled. "You can't accuse them of being nosy."

"Or else they play music so loud they couldn't hear over it," Amy said.

"A lion." He helped himself to some coleslaw. "One of my roommates had an iguana once. It escaped. We never did find out where it went."

They chatted on about nothing of importance. Being alone with Quent in the cozy kitchen at night, eating companionably and sharing anecdotes from the day, gave Amy a sensation of belonging.

When his outstretched leg bumped her ankle, a tremor of excitement ran up her spine. Every movement he made reverberated through her.

By the time she finished eating, Amy was contemplating ways to slip onto his lap. Better yet, she imagined him catching her as she moved toward the sink and drawing her into his arms.

He was watching her, no question about it. Awareness crackled between them.

"Why don't we—" she began.

"Amy," Quent said.

"Mmm?" She could scarcely breathe.

"We…what I'd like…" He searched for words. "What I want to do is to carry you down the hall and ravish you like a caveman, but…"

"Great!" she said.

"You mean that?"

"I'm not sure," she admitted, already regretting her impulsive response.

"I didn't think so." Across the table, Quent's blue

eyes were troubled. "I hate denying my instincts. It sure would feel right to make love to you."

"I heard a 'but,'" Amy said. "You'd better finish that sentence."

"Going to bed together would change everything. I want to do this right, when it happens." Then he added three words that chilled her. "If it happens."

Until now, she'd known Quent didn't love her, but she'd hoped that might change. Didn't physical intimacy, especially when accompanied by genuine liking, sometimes lead to much more?

"I thought about you all day," he went on. "I imagined what might happen tonight. In the past, I've taken things pretty casually with women, although I've never deliberately hurt anybody."

"You've decided to make an exception in my case?" she asked with what she hoped was light irony.

"About hurting you? Never," he said. "About taking it lightly, yes. You're special. I don't want to start something and maybe ruin it while we're adjusting to taking care of the children. Relationships can be tricky. We've both seen that in our parents' marriages."

That made sense, she conceded. At least he didn't claim to have lost his desire for her.

"Besides, you agreed to let me move in for the kids' sake, not to be your lover," Quent went on.

At this rate, she might still be a virgin when she was sixty! "Hey, what's the big deal?" Amy joked. "In my vast experience…"

He raised a hand to stop her. "I don't want to hear about your adventures with other guys, or how I fail to measure up to them, either."

She couldn't believe he had any doubts on that score. Maybe it was time, painful as it might be, to level with him. "The truth is, I'm not as experienced as you think."

"Whoa!" Quent rocked backward in his chair. "Please don't spoil my illusions. I like the fact that you know your way around. It's a turn-on."

"It is?" Oh, what a tangled web she had woven!

"You're my fantasy woman," he said. "Let's leave it at that, okay?"

"All right." There was no sense in belaboring the point, since he'd made it clear they weren't hopping into bed anytime soon. Amy couldn't bear to think about how disappointed he was going to be when they did.

If it happens, he'd said. Maybe it never would. She wasn't sure how she felt about that, after what he'd just told her.

"How about a game of darts?" Quent asked.

"You're on," she said, and proceeded to beat him two games out of three.

QUENT AWOKE to intense darkness. At his apartment, car lights sometimes flashed by on the street and the people in the next unit played the TV late. Here, all was stillness.

Then he heard the sound that must have penetrated his sleep. The murmur of voices in the hallway. Conditioned by years as a medical resident, he arose and went to see what was happening.

Only after his feet hit the floor did his body register stiffness from sleeping on a mattress that offered little protection from its metal frame. He shrugged it off.

In the hallway, the faint glow of a night-light cast shadows. Quent made out Greg's little shape as it disappeared into his bedroom, and Amy's, following.

He glimpsed her tangled dark hair and the eddying fabric of her gown. Guessing that his intrusion might interfere with getting the boy back to sleep, Quent waited in the semi-darkness.

Amy emerged sooner than expected and ran right into him. As he reached to steady her, her breasts nudged his arm. Through the gossamer fabric, her body pressed itself against his, each curve delineated with excruciating clarity.

They stepped back, both apologizing at once, then fell silent. Neither moved. In the lull, the rhythms of their breathing intertwined.

In Quent's fevered mind, his palms glided along the flare of her hips. He imagined her yielding as his palms stroked upwards, lifting the nightgown. Beneath it, she would be nude and breathtakingly lovely.

His lips tingled with the need to kiss her. All of her. It didn't matter how much experience Amy had, he was going to arouse sensations she'd never dreamed of, the same kind she inspired in him.

On the verge of reaching out, he hesitated as anxiety, like a miasma from an unseen swamp, swirled up without warning. It was overwhelming, this sense of an unnamed danger lurking in the shadows. Where had it come from?

There must be a reason why his subconscious was throwing up this alert, Quent thought. Maybe it was protecting him and Amy from his impulsive nature. He certainly didn't want to make a premature move that would annoy her.

He'd always believed that, if you let it, life fell into place. In the long run, everything would sort itself out. Frustrated but resigned, he refrained from touching her.

"Is everything okay?" he asked instead.

''I heard Greg get up.'' Amy's voice came out thick. She swallowed. ''He's fine.''

''Good night, then.''

''Good night.''

She slipped by. He felt her warmth linger in the cool air long after the bedroom door closed behind her.

ON SATURDAY, they went Christmas shopping, encouraging the children to identify toys for Santa to give them later. Amy found the vast selection almost overwhelming, and was grateful that the kids seemed to have a clear idea of what they wanted. Or at least in Tara's case, she knew how to point and say, ''Mine!''

She knew what she wanted for Christmas, but she wasn't likely to get it. These past two nights, her longing for Quent had tantalized every waking moment. Each time he came near, her pulse quickened and her skin registered the air currents as if they were caresses.

He wanted her, too, she was almost certain of it. Surely her instincts couldn't be entirely wrong. She respected his decision to hold back, however, or perhaps she was simply afraid to give up the safety of the known for a plunge into uncharted seas.

She returned her attention to the toy store. Quent was vetoing Greg's choice of a large box of Lego.

''Tara might swallow one of the pieces,'' he said. ''After all, you're sharing a room.''

''I'm tired of baby stuff!'' Greg retorted.

''He can store them in my room,'' Amy said. ''Tara's going to be a toddler for a couple more years. You can't expect Greg to play with blocks forever.''

''Good point,'' Quent conceded. ''We'll have to be careful about when and where they can be played with, though. Okay?''

"Sure," Greg said.

After the kids were in bed, Quent went back to purchase the selections, along with plenty of colorful paper. They wrapped the toys at the dining-room table and hid them in a closet.

He was so polite, Amy wanted to slap him. What had happened to her frisky playmate from the afternoon before the palm tree fell?

He'd grown up and become a father, she supposed. But why did his newfound maturity have to breed caution in every aspect of his life?

Well, not every aspect, she found to her relief. On Sunday afternoon, they spent hours at a playground, whooping and laughing. Greg tried to imitate the way his uncle walked and gestured. Tara enjoyed having "conversations" with Amy, even though many of her words remained unintelligible at this age.

Already, Amy could feel the bonds strengthening between her, Quent and the children. Bit by bit, they were becoming a family.

She and Quent were learning how to compromise, she realized. At the park, they couldn't find anywhere to wash hands. After a brief discussion, they decided to allow the children to wipe off the dirt on their clothing before eating the snack they'd brought. Quent promised to buy a pocket-size bottle of hand sanitizer, which Amy had never heard of before.

When it was time to go, Greg refused to leave. Although she would have preferred that he learn to obey the rules without quarreling, Amy smoothed matters over by reminding him of a TV show he wanted to watch.

"We can't expect them to be perfect," she said once

they were home, with Tara napping and Greg, having tired of the TV program, throwing darts at the board.

"As a physician, I'd rather they lived in a sterile environment, ate only health food and never watched TV," Quent admitted over a cup of hot chocolate. "That's not realistic, I can see."

"They'd be miserable and so would we," she agreed.

"Let's be honest. I'm the original junk-food junkie, and there's nothing like a kung-fu movie on late-night television." He helped himself to a cookie. "Being responsible for a child's well-being sure changes my perspective."

"I've got a lot to learn, too," Amy said. "It didn't occur to me to keep Greg's toys stored where Tara can't reach them. I'm glad you brought it up."

"We make a good team." He offered her the cookies, and she took one.

"Yes, we do." She tried not to dwell on how much she wanted them to be a real team.

Several times over the weekend, Amy had noticed Quent watching her with a warm expression. He'd rushed to steady her when she'd nearly fallen off the monkey bars at the playground, and she'd leaned against him, relishing his strength and protection. He hadn't been in any hurry to separate from her, either.

There was hope yet, she supposed.

NATALIE, her face tanned from her cruise, gave a thumbs-up after tasting her salad at the Birthing Center cafeteria. "The menu has improved by leaps and bounds. Sun-dried tomatoes and feta cheese at Doctors Circle! Who could have imagined?"

"With an ambience like this, I'd be tempted to eat

here every day, except that I'd gain weight." Heather took another bite of her fettuccine with pesto sauce.

Amy's gaze swept the redecorated room. As part of the center's remodeling, the drab cafeteria had been repainted, the linoleum replaced and French-style glass doors installed at the entrance to the patio. There was a new menu, too.

"They could have done more with the holiday decorations." She made a face at the scattering of cranberry-red bows that were the only sign of the season. "I realize that Christmas colors clash with the new palette, but what's wrong with excess?"

"I must be dining with the wrong Amy Ravenna," Natalie said. "Didn't you tell me last year that you hated all the fuss and that ornaments should be banned unless they're edible?"

Amy squirmed, wishing she could take back that Scrooge-like sentiment. "I was on an environmental kick. Besides, that was before…"

"Before you had kids," Heather finished for her. "Along with a live-in boyfriend who likes to party."

"He's not my boyfriend," Amy said. "And now that he's a father, he's only interested in the kind of party that comes with balloons and birthday cakes."

"When are you going to stop pretending this is strictly platonic?" Natalie teased. "We weren't born yesterday, you know."

"Don't start!" She cringed at how far her friends were from the truth. True to his word, Quent hadn't given her so much as a good-night kiss all weekend. "You just got back today and already you're on my case."

"I ran into Mrs. McLanahan this morning while I was making rounds," Heather said. "She was delivering a gift-shop bouquet. The moment she saw me, she started humming a wedding march.''

"Obviously she thinks you're getting married," Amy said. "Although I can't imagine why."

"As she passed me, she said, 'Tell your friend those kids need a permanent mom.' I think she was referring to you," Heather said.

Amy sighed. Obviously the grapevine had reached Noreen big-time.

"It'll turn into a romance," Natalie said sympathetically. "You want it to, don't you?"

More than she could possibly express. More than she even dared think about. "He's a lost cause," she said. "Quent sees me as his best buddy, nothing more."

"You think not?" A small pucker formed between Heather's eyebrows. "I've watched you two together. Take it from a grandma, there's lava bubbling beneath the still waters."

"Speaking of water!" Natalie smacked her palms on the table. "You and your families are invited to a party on Patrick's yacht Christmas Eve. I mean, Patrick's and my yacht."

"You're entertaining on the boat?" The prospect pleased Amy. Every Christmas, residents of the mansions lining the harbor set up lighting arrays. The moored boats were usually decorated, too. Judging from photographs she'd seen in the newspaper, it made a splendid sight, all that brilliance reflecting on the water. "May we bring our kids?"

"Of course!" Her friend grinned, enjoying her new role as hostess. She was staying on as Patrick's secretary, too, until the baby was born. "I have to admit, it's not entirely social."

"Another fund-raiser?" Heather asked.

''More like a reward for our supporters,'' Nat said. ''Loretta suggested it.''

The public relations director was always seeking ways to encourage the patrons of Doctors Circle. She'd regained her old energy and verve in the weeks since her last counseling session, Amy was glad to note. She was especially grateful for this latest idea.

The cruise was sure to be the icing on the cake. This year, she already knew the holidays would be extra-special because of the children.

On Christmas, which was only ten days off, she and Quent had talked about inviting Lucy and the grandparents to dinner. That would be fun, and Quent could try out his new cooking skills. Last night, after consulting with Aunt Mary on child-friendly menus, he'd broiled hamburgers and made mashed potatoes, the instant kind.

Her chin resting on her palm, she began planning the menu. Ham or turkey? Sweet potatoes and cranberry sauce, of course, and two or three kinds of pie. Knowing Quent, she figured he'd prefer three.

From the corner of her eye, she caught Natalie and Heather exchanging a knowing smile. Her friends obviously figured she was dreaming about Quent. Well, in a way, she was.

That evening, Amy stayed late to meet with a new mother suffering from postpartum depression. Talking about her feelings of being overwhelmed clearly helped. Also, the young mom agreed to keep a diary about her emotions and to hire a cleaning service to come in once a month and do the heavy work.

Amy arrived home eager to tell Quent and the kids about the yacht party. When she opened the door, she saw that they weren't the only ones waiting for her.

Lucy, looking unusually formal in a tailored suit, perched on the edge of an armchair.

"This is a nice surprise!" Amy said. Then she spotted Quent standing to one side with arms folded and storm clouds gathering in his eyes.

"It's not so nice, I'm afraid," Lucy said. "I'm being transferred to our Kansas City office. I've thought it over, and I've decided to take the children with me."

Chapter Thirteen

In the stunned silence, through Amy's mind flashed images of the children at breakfast, of yesterday's outing to the park, of the tree she and Quent planned to decorate for Christmas. In such a short time, Greg and Tara had become a major part of her life.

Her hearing, keenly attuned to the youngsters, picked up happy noises coming from their bedroom. Thank goodness neither had any idea that their fate was being decided out here in the living room.

She could see from Quent's expression that he meant to fight, but Lucy was their legal guardian. Surely they could find a better solution than battling this out in court.

Carefully, Amy said, "I'm sorry you're leaving. But won't it be even more difficult to relocate with two small children?"

"Believe me, I'm not looking forward to it." Lucy avoided Quent's glare.

"Please tell me why you've changed your mind." She eased onto the couch.

Lucy shifted uneasily in her chair. "My company just opened an office in Kansas City. Another employee was supposed to be transferred, but he quit to take a different

job, so I got picked," she said. "It's a step up for me
and I can't afford to turn it down."

"I can understand that, but..." Quent paused when
Lucy's back stiffened. Obviously, the two of them had
already crossed swords, and he was wise enough not to
make a bad situation worse.

"When do you have to leave?" Amy forced herself
to maintain a neutral tone.

"Right after the first of the year." Lucy finger-
combed her short, dark-blond hair, leaving it rumpled.
"They told me on Friday. After thinking about it all
weekend, I decided I'm still responsible to my sister for
making sure the children are okay. As long as I was
close enough to visit, I could do that, but now I'll be
too far away."

"This works both ways," Quent pointed out. "If
they're in Kansas City, I won't be able to visit them
regularly, either."

"We could get one of those video-conferencing pro-
grams for the computer," Amy told Lucy. "You could
see them and talk to them as often as you like."

"I appreciate that, but it's not the same thing." Obviously torn, she gestured around her. "You've got a
nice place, and it seems as if everything's working out.
Still, my conscience won't let me run off and leave
them. Who knows what will happen? I don't mean to
be negative, but people can easily break off engagements. With Quent's hours at the clinic, he couldn't take
care of them by himself."

"We aren't going to break up," he said.

Although Amy's instincts urged her to agree, she
didn't want to be any more dishonest than they'd already been. She waited silently for the response.

"You can't be sure. I know you two met after Quent

moved here, and that was only a few months ago. You've known each other such a short time, you might decide not to get married.'' Lucy stood up. ''I'm sorry this is so disruptive for the kids. It's better to get it over with quickly, so I'll pick them up Saturday.''

''I've got an idea,'' Quent said.

Both women regarded him questioningly. ''What is it?'' Lucy said.

''I'd like to discuss it with Amy.'' He took a deep breath. ''Can I call you tomorrow?''

''Sure.'' Although Lucy sounded puzzled, she didn't press him. ''Believe me, I wish there were some other way. The kids seem happy here and it's going to be tough in a new place. I have an obligation to my sister's memory, though.''

''Of course you do,'' Amy said.

''I'll call you,'' Quent told their guest. ''Please understand that I appreciate how much you care about the kids. I don't know what would have happened if you hadn't been there a year ago.''

''That's why I took them.'' Lucy went to say goodbye to Tara and Greg, with hugs all around. When she returned, she collected her pocketbook. ''I'll talk to you tomorrow.''

''Count on it,'' Quent said.

Amy could hardly wait for the door to close behind her before bursting out, ''What's your idea?'' She hoped it was a good one. How could either of them bear to lose Tara and Greg?

''Let's eat supper first.'' He started for the kitchen. ''The kids must be starving. Besides, I've got a few details to think about before we discuss it.''

She couldn't imagine what he had in mind that would

persuade Lucy to alter her plans. He'd have to be some kind of magician. Well, she'd find out soon enough.

Dinner proved a pleasant distraction. Quent made spaghetti and sauce. Served with garlic bread and salad, it won Greg's approval, and Tara downed almost as much spaghetti as she smeared on her face. Instead of salad, she ate mashed peas, which added to the mess.

"Wearing makeup already?" Quent joked afterwards as he mopped his niece with a washcloth. "I have to say, you did a thorough job of applying it."

Greg carried his plastic plate to the sink for Amy. "See? I'm a big boy. I can help."

"Thank you," she said. "I don't know what I'd do without you." She meant it.

As they finished cleaning, she remembered about Natalie and Patrick's yacht party. Unless Quent's idea worked, the children wouldn't be there. She wanted so much for them all to be together at Christmas.

They bathed the children and read to them. After Greg said his prayers, he and Tara fell asleep quickly.

"Follow me," Quent whispered, and led the way into Amy's office, where he was staying. From the closet, he removed one of his white coats.

"What's this for?"

"I want to check something." With a deft motion, he draped the coat over her hair and shoulders, then stepped back to admire his handiwork. "Hmm, very nice."

Amy felt ridiculous. At the same time, she was tempted to dart across the hall and examine herself in her new full-length mirror to find out what he found so fascinating. "What's very nice?"

"You look good in white." Amusement colored Quent's face. "That's the important thing."

"For what?"

"A bride," he said.

Amy's cheeks got hot, then cold. She hoped she wasn't changing colors like a chameleon. "I am not going through a mock wedding to fool Lucy!"

"Who said anything about a mock wedding?" Quent pressed one hand to his chest as if she'd wounded him. "I would never pull something like that."

"Oh? What about our mock engagement?" she asked.

"That was different."

"How?"

"An engagement is in the mind of the beholder," Quent said. "A marriage is a matter of legal record."

"That's a twisted way of thinking. In any case, I hope you're joking." After removing the coat, Amy handed it back.

He hung it away. "Not at all. Seriously, we ought to get married."

She'd dreamed about Quent proposing to her, but not under these circumstances. He didn't love her, he simply wanted a marriage of convenience. Amy's lungs squeezed so tight they hurt.

When she spoke, she forced herself to keep her tone light. "How romantic. Usually when men propose to me, they get down on their knees and beg."

He frowned. "How many men have asked you to marry them?"

"I lost count." Amy hadn't expected him to take her remark at face value. "Oh, come on, you can't mean it. We're not even dating!"

"Think about it. It makes perfect sense." He glanced around the office. "Wait. There's nowhere comfortable to sit in here while we talk."

''We could go in the kitchen.'' On second thought, that wasn't such a good idea. He might decide to pelt her with rice to see if he liked that effect.

''The dining room,'' he said. ''My parents always had their serious discussions over the big table.''

''Then let's do it.'' Amy certainly didn't want to stay here, where the only places to sit were a desk chair and his bed.

At the dining table, they took chairs at right angles, around a corner from each other. Quent had such a businesslike air that, for one wild moment, Amy half-expected him to whip out a notebook and begin listing reasons why getting married was a sensible idea. If he did, she was going to slap him.

''Before we start,'' she said, ''are you talking about a temporary marriage? Because I'd never agree to that.'' She stopped, unwilling to admit aloud what a mockery it would make of her dreams.

Quent folded his strong hands on the table. A thin white scar stood out where, he'd explained once, he'd cut himself with a scalpel while in medical school.

''It's such a new idea, I haven't thought it through,'' he conceded. ''I wasn't figuring we'd run out afterwards and get a divorce, if that's what you're worried about.''

Although Amy knew that many marriages broke up, including that of her parents, she could never be cynical about a sacred union. Especially not her own. ''You still make it sound awfully casual. For me, marriage is forever.''

Once she claimed Quent in bed, or he claimed her, or they lost control and ravished each other, she could never go back to being friends. There was a level of intimacy that, once achieved, had to be honored and cherished.

"Forever? That's a tall order." Quent regarded her through a rebellious lock of blond hair that had fallen across his forehead. "There are no guarantees. Still, we have so much in common, the odds would be on our side."

"You have a bizarre attitude," Amy said. "One minute you're fooling around draping a coat over my head. The next thing I know, you're dissecting our chances of living happily ever after as if marriage were some kind of lab experiment."

"I don't have a grand theory of matrimony. I admit it." Half in jest, he added, "Why don't you explain it to me?"

"People who get married are supposed to fall in love." Amy gestured helplessly with her hands. "They don't plan it, they get carried away by their feelings."

"That might happen to us someday, but we can't afford to wait," Quent said. "If we do, we'll lose the kids."

"I know, but..."

He pressed on. "The way I see it, most of my friends who've gotten married did it more or less the way you described, yielding to their impulses instead of their intellects. Sometimes things worked and sometimes they didn't."

"That's the risk you have to take," Amy said.

"I'm more analytical than that." This was the doctor side of him speaking, she could see; not her usual fun-loving companion but the man who'd patiently advised a roomful of teenagers about child development. "What we have are solid underpinnings, and I don't think we need to wait and hope our emotions will knock us off our feet before January."

Amy gathered her patience. "Like what solid under-pinnings?"

"First of all, you're a natural mom." His expression warmed. "You've really taken to the kids and they adore you. We could make a happy home for them."

Birthday parties and balloons. Summer outings to the beach. The first day of school, soccer and scouts, senior proms. Amy ached to share all of those with Greg and Tara. And, most of all, with Quent.

"I know we're buddies," he went on, "but isn't that the key? We're attracted to each other. At least, I'm definitely attracted to you, and I think it's mutual, although I may not be as suave as some of the studs you've dated."

She nearly burst out laughing, turning it into a cough at the last minute. "Don't be too hard on yourself."

"We have a good time and we can talk to each other." Quent seemed to be trying to persuade himself more than her. "Amy, I've been happier this past week than I've ever been. I know I'm younger than you, but I'm turning thirty next month. I'm sure I can live up to your standards."

He looked so earnest and sweet, Amy couldn't resist him. She yearned to be his wife more than anything in the world, and she'd always believed in her father's advice to go after what she wanted. Maybe this whole business would blow up in her face, but she had to take the chance, for Quent, for the children and for herself.

"Sure," she said. "Why not?"

It took a few blinks for him to absorb her response. "Yes? You'll marry me?" He let out a whoop.

"The kids!" Amy protested.

"Sorry." He calmed down. "I forgot they were sleeping."

They paused to listen, but no one called from the bedroom. "Solid sleepers," Amy said.

"Lucky for us. Now let's seal our bargain, shall we?" Without waiting for an answer, Quent pulled her toward him across the edge of the table. Their mouths met for a brief, tantalizing kiss.

In another minute, Amy knew she'd be tugging him down the hall to her bedroom, as she'd dreamed of doing all week. There were too many plans to make. Besides, since she'd waited this long, she might as well be a virgin when she walked down the aisle.

Okay, she admitted silently, maybe she was a little apprehensive, too. What was Quent going to say when he found out she'd invented all that worldly experience? She had no idea. Apparently, she was going to find out—on her wedding night.

"We haven't finished talking," she said, pulling back.

Reluctantly, he released her. "I'm listening."

"Since Lucy already thinks we're engaged, I doubt she'll change her mind about taking the kids simply because we announce we're getting married."

"That's right. We need to set a date." Quent glanced at his watch, the digital kind with a built-in calendar. "She's leaving right after the first of the year. How about the weekend before New Year's?"

"I want to make sure the children can spend Christmas with us," Amy said. "What if Lucy insists on taking them until we prove we're going through with it?"

"Agreed." Quent gave her a conspiratorial grin. "I guess we should say our vows right away. What are you doing on Saturday?"

Saturday? That was so soon! "We were going to spend the day buying a tree," Amy blurted, then shook her head at her own reaction. "I didn't mean to raise objections. But it's so sudden."

"I'm afraid the calendar isn't very forgiving," said the man who, unless she'd hallucinated this entire conversation, had just promised to become her husband.

"Okay." Amy decided to go with the flow and let her psyche handle the repercussions in due course. "I used to think I wanted to elope, but after Natalie's wedding, I changed my mind."

"We won't have time to arrange anything big." Quent touched her hand, sending a soft glow through Amy. "That doesn't mean we can't do something special. Tell me what you want."

"A romantic setting. Lots of friends," she said. "Aunt Mary always knows what to do." She started to laugh.

"What's so funny?"

"We won't have to worry about hiring an organist!" she said. "Mrs. McLanahan's been humming a wedding march since you moved in with me. All we have to do is invite her, and she'll provide the music."

"Let's hire a pianist and let Noreen entertain at the reception," he said, deadpan.

"She'll be so excited, she'll probably dance, too." Amy toyed with her French braid, which was coming apart. "A wedding! On Saturday! There are so many details to work out, I don't know where to start."

From his pocket, Quent pulled his personal organizer. "How about the guest list?"

"It's as good a place as any."

ACT NOW, deal with the consequences later. The motto was standing him in good stead, Quent reflected the next day as he dialed Lucy's work number during his lunch break.

He was glad he'd asked Amy to marry him, and even more pleased that she'd said yes. Surely they could find a way to make this work, to keep it light, to give each other space and avoid whatever imaginary abyss kept giving him the willies.

Everything would be fine as long as Lucy agreed they could keep the children. He didn't want to wait until the end of the day to talk to her. This was too important.

In the privacy of his book-lined office, Quent listened to the phone ringing at the other end of the line. When Lucy answered, he said, "Dr. Quentin Ladd and Dr. Amy Ravenna request the honor of your presence at their wedding on Saturday."

"You mean it?" she asked.

"I do," he said. "I mean, we do. Or rather, we both plan to say 'I do.'"

"Wow!" Relief filled Lucy's voice. "That's wonderful news."

"The children can stay with us, then?" He didn't take it for granted, because he knew what a strong bond had formed between her and their mutual niece and nephew.

Lucy let out a long breath. "Part of me wants to keep them. I love those little guys. If things were different, I'd never let them go. But as matters stand, that wouldn't be fair to anybody."

"You'll always be welcome to visit whenever you want," Quent said.

"Believe me, I'll take you up on that." Excitedly, Lucy went on. "A wedding! I hope I'm not spoiling your plans by rushing you this way."

"The important thing is that the children will have a permanent home," he said.

"If you'll hire a lawyer, we can start the adoption proceedings. I guess there'll be some kind of home study like I had, but I'm sure it will be fine," she said. "Congratulations, Quent. I always knew you'd make a great father when you grew up. The question was, how long would that take?"

"A few months ago, I wouldn't have bet on it happening soon," he said. "I've changed since I came to Serene Beach."

"Amy changed you," Lucy said.

"You're right about that."

After they hung up, he sat staring into space. Marriage. The dark shadowy sense of danger was still there, still cautioning him about how disastrously wrong things could go.

So what? he thought. He and Amy weren't their parents. They were two intelligent, loving people. Most of all, they were pals.

There was no reason why they couldn't live happily ever after more as friends and lovers than as a conventional husband and wife. They'd already made a good start at it.

And he had no doubt the best was yet to come.

STANDING AT THE GLASS counter in the jewelry store, Amy hesitated to try on the ring. The swirl of diamonds captured the fantasy she'd treasured since girlhood so perfectly that she was afraid it wouldn't fit, and that, if it didn't, it couldn't be sized in time for the wedding.

Mostly, she was afraid this moment wasn't really happening.

"Want me to slip it on you?" Without waiting for an answer, Quent took her hand and lifted the ring.

Amy's breath caught. His blond head as he gazed downward made her feel like Cinderella waiting for the prince to try on the glass slipper. Even though she knew it was *her* glass slipper, there was always the possibility that the magic couldn't be trusted.

"It's a new design. We just started carrying the line," said the elderly jeweler, Hugo Oldham, a friend of Mrs. McLanahan's who owned several shops. "I discovered the designer last month."

"Just in time." Cupping her palm in his, Quent slid the ring along Amy's finger. It stopped at her knuckle, stirring a breath of disappointment before he twitched it free. "See? It's exactly right."

Depths glinted in the diamonds and in Quent's eyes as he watched her reaction. He kept her hand in his with subtle possessiveness, his skin ruddy against Amy's olive hue.

"It was made for us," she said.

"Never let her go," Hugo told Quent.

"I don't intend to."

It was at that moment that Amy began to trust that maybe, just maybe, the magic might be real.

IN THE MIRROR of her old room at Aunt Mary's house, she studied herself. She'd chosen an ivory cocktail dress that flattered her dark hair and eyes. The silky way it swished around her legs felt sexy.

"You look gorgeous." Heather tucked an errant flower into the wreath atop Amy's head.

"I'm glad you agreed to be my maid of honor on such short notice." Her friend's presence steadied her. Aunt Mary was busy watching the children, and Natalie, although honored, had declined to be a bridesmaid due to her pregnancy.

"I'm a practical woman. I like getting to use my dress twice." Heather smoothed down the turquoise outfit she'd worn at Natalie's ceremony only two weeks earlier.

Amy appreciated the acceptance and the discretion of her two best friends since she'd made her surprise announcement. At work, the grapevine had gone crazy with speculation. The consensus, she'd heard, was that, as a friend, she was generously helping Quent with his niece and nephew.

Some people admired her. Others thought she'd taken leave of her senses. Mercifully, neither Natalie nor Heather had breathed a word of what must be obvious to them, that Amy was head over heels in love, even if Quent wasn't.

Thank goodness Heather, aware that Amy hadn't had any reason to use contraception in the past, had helped her arrange for it now. There was a lot to be said for having a doctor as one of her best friends!

The week had passed in a whirl. Aunt Mary, overjoyed that Amy had found the right man to marry, had gamely organized her friends to decorate the house and cook for the reception.

On such short notice, they'd invited only about thirty intimates, including, of course, Noreen. Almost everyone had been happy to come. Amy's father and one of her brothers had driven down from Fresno, while Lucy had arrived with Quent's father from San Diego.

Amy snapped out of her reflections as Kitty came in wearing the aqua bridesmaid dress she'd borrowed from Amy. It fit better than expected, although Aunt Mary had had to tack up the hem.

Her aunt deserved a medal. Amy made a mental note to throw a big thank-you party to celebrate Mary's fiftieth birthday next fall.

Behind Kitty strode Loretta, who'd volunteered to record the event on film. As the P.R. director at Doctors Circle, she knew how to take professional-quality photographs.

After a few obligatory shots of the bride with her attendants, Loretta shuttered her camera. "Good luck," she said. "I don't know anyone who deserves happiness more than you, Amy."

"Thank you." Amy reached out and squeezed the other woman's free hand.

"I'm glad these children are going to have a great mom," Loretta said. "I'm amazed how quickly you've bonded with them."

"It surprises me, too," she said.

"Speaking of the kids, we'd better go downstairs." Kitty paced to and fro in excitement. "Tara's starting to squirm and Lucy says she won't be able to keep her quiet forever."

"Let's do it!" Amy shooed her band of friends ahead of her out of the room. "One wedding, coming up."

When she saw her father waiting in the upstairs hall, Amy's heart began to hammer in her chest. This was really happening. In a few minutes, she was going to marry Quent.

For better or for worse.

Chapter Fourteen

In the high-ceilinged living room, butterfly-shaped balloons danced on their tethers above masses of ruffly paper flowers. To the guests in their folding chairs, it must seem as if they were sitting in a garden, Quent thought.

"You haven't lost the ring yet, have you?" he teased Greg. The little boy, garbed in a new suit, shook his head solemnly.

"I'll make sure he doesn't." Gary Lee, Quent's best man and a close friend from medical school, stood with one hand resting lightly on the ring bearer's shoulder. "He's a very responsible young fellow, so I'm sure we don't have to worry."

A glow of satisfaction spread through Quent as he glanced from the fresh-faced child to Tara, a yellow bow askew in her hair as she played with a simple puzzle in the front row beside Lucy. He'd already found a lawyer and begun the home study. Soon he and Amy would be their parents in every sense of the word.

To his right, the minister indicated to the pianist to segue from love songs into a march. Both the pastor and the woman at the piano had come from Aunt

Mary's church, kindly rearranging their plans to accommodate the last-minute affair.

When the tempo altered, Kitty appeared on the staircase with a single white rose in her hand. She strolled down at a measured pace, looking thrilled and a bit shy. Quent had to remind himself that this blushing teenager was about to become his cousin. Marrying meant acquiring a whole new family!

Heather followed, her back straight, her hands graceful on her rose. She exchanged a smile with Natalie, who sat watching dreamily beside her new husband.

It occurred to Quent that he should have slipped the pianist an extra twenty to speed up the procession. He could hardly wait to see Amy, who had refused to show him her dress in advance.

After an eon, he heard the strains of "Here Comes the Bride." Down the staircase floated Amy on her father's arm. Loretta moved forward to snap a few shots before taking her seat.

The first thing Quent noticed about his bride-to-be were her legs, nicely displayed by the elegant dress. She had great calves, long and slim. All brides ought to wear mid-length gowns if they looked as good in them as Amy did.

The lacy fabric swished tantalizingly around her knees and clung to her slender waist. Spaghetti straps showed off her bare shoulders, and through her dark hair wove a magical array of flowers and silver sparkles.

A soft light diffused across her face. Quent's breath caught in his throat. Radiant, that's how she looked.

Even if he hadn't rehearsed the night before, he would instinctively have stepped forward and offered his arm. Behind him, he heard the pastor ask, "Who gives this woman to be married?"

"I do." Pride beamed from her father as he handed over his daughter.

The rest of the ceremony blurred in Quent's mind. All he could focus on was Amy. Her light perfume awakened images of canopied beds and silken sheets, yet there was an air of innocence about her today, too. Something about a wedding transformed the bride into a young girl about to experience love for the first time.

What would it be like if he were the man to awaken her? To be her first lover, her entire world of experience? Quent couldn't imagine. Besides, he preferred Amy the way she was.

He stirred from his reverie to accept the ring from Greg. With only a slight tug, it slid onto Amy's finger, where the diamonds twinkled like living stars.

"Wow!" the little boy said loudly, then clapped his hand over his mouth. An amused murmur rose from their guests.

"It's okay," Amy told the child in a stage whisper. "I think it's pretty, too."

After they said their vows, they turned to face their friends with Greg between them. Tara, who'd grown wiggly on her chair, squirmed onto the floor and toddled over.

"I now present to you Dr. and Mrs. Ladd, and children," said the minister.

Applause erupted. Quent scooped up his daughter, Amy took Greg's hand, and down the aisle they went.

On any other occasion, he'd have relished the surge of friends and the delicious food in the dining room. You'd have had to pry him away with a crowbar.

Today, he wanted to whisk Amy out to his flower-trimmed SUV. It was a two-hour drive to their hotel in Palm Springs, and he could hardly wait.

WEDDING-NIGHT JITTERS. Thirty-three-year-old women weren't supposed to get them. Especially not if they were marriage counselors.

Amy knew the facts. What she didn't know was how they were going to get from point A to point B, or how Quent would react when he discovered his smart-talking bride was clueless in the bedroom.

The advantage of wearing a cocktail dress was that she didn't have to put on fresh clothes before they left the reception. Otherwise, judging by Quent's eagerness to get her alone, she suspected he'd have trotted upstairs and insisted on helping her change. As it was, he sent Kitty to fetch her suitcase, bade everyone farewell as soon as politeness allowed, and broke the speed limit all the way to Palm Springs.

"I'm sure the kids will have a great time with Aunt Mary," Amy said as they waited for the registration clerk to process his credit card. "She's going to take them to an amusement park tomorrow."

"Did I mention how much I like those flowers in your hair?" In his dark suit, Quent looked dashing. And sexy. And incredibly romantic. "I love when you wear it loose that way, like a cloud."

"You can brush it out for me." The image of him touching and stroking her made Amy's stockings feel too tight. She searched for a topic more suitable to discuss in a hotel lobby. "It was nice of Dr. Fingger to cover for you this weekend."

"I have to return the favor by being on call after ten o'clock Christmas Eve," Quent said. "Don't worry, we'll be able to go to the Barrs' yacht party." He ran a finger across her cheekbone, sending shimmers down

Amy's spine. Every instinct urged her to fling her arms around him and cuddle up close. Very close.

"Here you are, sir." The clerk returned the credit card. "Would you like a porter?"

"That won't be necessary." Quent accepted their keys and hoisted his bag along with Amy's. They'd packed lightly, since they were only staying one night. On such short notice, it had been impossible to steal even one extra day from a workweek already shortened by the Christmas holiday.

They'd make up for their abbreviated honeymoon next summer. Quent had offered to take her to Hawaii for a whole week. His expectations of marriage might not be traditional, Amy reflected, but they were definitely amorous.

When he escorted her into their room, she gave a little cry of appreciation. "It's a suite. How beautiful!"

Pale pastel fabrics swathed an outer chamber furnished with low couches and a cozy dining table. The creamy carpet ended at a set of steps that led up to a whirlpool spa, ready for action beside a pile of white towels. The bedroom lay beyond, out of sight. But not out of mind.

"Only the best for my wife," Quent said. "Wait a minute. I want to carry you in."

"I'm kind of tall for that, aren't I?" she asked regretfully. "I don't want my groom spraining his back before we get to first base."

"What do you take me for, a wimp?" After flinging their bags inside, Quent whipped around and picked her up. Amy clung to him, enjoying his strength. She wished she could lie here forever, suspended next to this wonderful, unpredictable man.

He stepped across the threshold and held her for a moment, his mouth brushing hers with a promise of more to come. Amy wanted it right now.

Quent set her down as lightly as if she were made of gossamer. "How did I do?"

"Magnificently."

She wished he'd take her back into his arms. Thirty-three years of waiting were coalescing into an intense longing to become Quent's wife in every way, right this instant.

He, however, seemed more interested in exploring their suite, especially after he spotted champagne cooling in a bucket. "I propose a toast. To best friends becoming lovers."

"You don't need to get me drunk for that!" Amy didn't want to come right out and tell him to forget the champagne, though, when he'd obviously gone to so much trouble to please her.

He set to work opening the bottle. "No headlong rush for my beautiful bride. I want this night to be unforgettable."

How could she argue with that? "Champagne sounds fabulous." Tamping down her impatience, Amy curled on the couch and prepared to let Quent wine and dine her.

A WOMAN'S wedding night was extremely important. Despite his eagerness to make steamy, nonstop love to Amy, Quent was determined to do this right, and that meant paying attention to details.

After making sure of her preferences, he'd ordered a meal of seafood and baby vegetables, scalloped potatoes, crusty French bread and a salad with raspberry dressing, plus a fine selection of tortes for dessert. Romantic music played from the stereo system as they were served in the privacy of their room by a waiter who knew how to keep his presence unobtrusive.

After the man left them alone, Quent switched on the jets in the spa and went into the bathroom to don his swimming trunks. He wanted to arouse Amy gradually, as she was no doubt accustomed to. The hints she'd dropped had given him the picture of a woman who expected skill and artfulness from her men.

It wasn't going to be easy to take it slow. All afternoon, he'd become more and more attuned to her femininity, her responsiveness, her sweetness. He had to keep a tight grip on himself tonight or risk disappointing her.

When he emerged, Quent found his new bride already in the spa. He nearly choked as he noticed her lacy peach bra and matching panties. The lingerie looked great on her, even better than he'd dreamed.

What a slim figure she had, its hint of shy sensuality forming an alluring contrast to her athletic tone. His wife was going to be full of surprises, Quent suspected, and he could hardly wait to discover them.

He eased into the pool across from her. If he stretched out his legs, he could tangle them with hers.

Take it easy, buster. You've got to watch yourself or you'll rip those skimpy clothes off her.

"I didn't think to bring a swimsuit." Amy gave him a mysterious smile. "I hope you don't mind if I wear this."

He cleared his throat. "I don't mind at all."

Heat surged around them. The swirling water caressed her breasts and fanned her hair across the ripples. The woman was a born temptress, Quent thought, closing his eyes and hovering near the edge of meltdown.

"You know," Amy said in a throaty voice, "I don't think people are required to wear anything at all in a spa."

"I didn't see any rules posted." With a grin, he dared to regard her again.

She leaned forward, dark tendrils playing around her breasts. Her gaze met his, daring him to make the next move.

Quent reached to finger a long strand and pulled her gently toward him. Amy's tongue touched her lips in what almost appeared to be hesitation. She was attuned to the most alluring subtleties, he thought admiringly.

At such close range, he could almost taste her. Was she as eager as he was? Or might she be mentally critiquing his style? He'd better play it safe.

"You must be stiff from the drive." He slipped one arm around Amy, offering his shoulder as a pillow. "Let's relax for a while."

"I don't want to relax. Do you?" She placed one palm against his chest and sighed as if thrilled by the mere sensation of touching him. Slowly she stroked downward, closer and closer to his rapidly responding male core. "Kiss me," she whispered.

Catching her waist, Quent swirled her onto his lap and slanted a kiss onto her luscious mouth. Amy kissed him back, long and deep. If she kept this up, he'd be all over her in a few seconds, and what would she think of him then?

Keeping a tight rein on his masculine drive, Quent lifted his head and smiled lazily. "What next? I want to do this your way."

"Well…" After nibbling her lip for a moment, Amy slid the bra strap off one shoulder and, catching his other hand, held it to her breast. The nub was hard and responsive. "Is this what you mean?"

"It's perfect." He eased off the other strap and cupped both breasts. Instantly, Quent's body hardened into one long lustful ache. The most exciting part was Amy's rapt expression, as if she were already in ecstasy.

Seeing her so lost in the moment, he trailed kisses along her neck and seized each nipple in turn between his lips. Moans tore from her, intensifying his desire. The moment Quent released her, she shot him a look of pure mischief and pulled off her panties, which she tossed onto the tile. "How's that?"

"Oh, sweetheart." He could hardly talk.

"Guess I'm doing okay so far, huh?"

"Better than okay. Better than…never mind."

The last shred of restraint vanished. Quent was yanking off his trunks when his bride pushed him onto the bench and straddled him. The warm, billowing water cushioned their movements.

"Hey, you caught me off guard!" he said with a smile. "I was going to do that to you first."

"I always wanted to win a wrestling match with you," Amy murmured close to his ear.

"Honey, you can win every match from now on."

He loved the way she knelt atop him, caressing his skin and sliding her body over his. "You're really, really good at this," he rasped.

"Am I?"

"As if you didn't know!" He smoothed his hands down to her rounded derriere and pulled her against his hardness. "I'm not sure how much longer I can hold out."

"Who asked you to?" Her laugh had a low, sexy hoarseness.

Quent played one palm lightly across Amy's heated center. Hungrily, she opened herself to him.

With pleasure so keen it bordered on agony, he

pressed inside her. Oddly, he felt a moment of resistance, but it scarcely registered before he claimed her.

Amy gasped. Quent, too, let out a moan as her enticing movements inflamed him. He drew her along him, in and out, and she caught his rhythm, quickening it almost to the point of no return. Abruptly, she stopped.

"Too fast," she whispered.

"I'm afraid you're right."

Kneeling on the narrow bench, Amy straightened herself atop Quent with him still inside her. She was heart-stoppingly beautiful, like a nymph as her bare breasts and narrow waist broke clear of the foam.

Even Quent's imagination hadn't prepared him for the splendor of making love with her. She'd brought a lifetime of experience to their marriage, and he relished it.

Above him, Amy began to sway. "This is amazing," she said.

"Good," he said. "Let's do it some more."

"I don't know how I survived without it."

"You never made love in a spa before?" Quent asked.

She shook her head.

"Neither did I." He groaned, because she'd reached down and taken him in her hands below their joining. When she heightened her movements, rational thought disappeared.

Grasping her hips, Quent plunged upward. Suffused in heat, he thrust into Amy until she gave a shudder of pure pleasure. Volcanic satisfaction erupted through him, again and again, while time froze into an eternal instant of bliss.

Gradually, as they half-floated in the swirling water, rapture faded into languor. Sinking onto the bench beside him, Amy leaned back. "I never realized it could be like that."

"Really?" Quent was glad their connection had been as exhilarating for her as it had for him. "Arrogant as I am, I still wasn't sure I'd live up to your expectations."

"It hurt a little at first, but Heather warned me…" She stopped at seeing his startled expression.

"What do you mean?" Quent tried to make sense of her words. "Heather warned you about what?"

"You didn't realize I was a virgin? I thought it was obvious."

His brain, befogged by champagne and great sex, slowly slotted the pieces into place. The initial resistance. Her wondering aloud how she'd lived without this.

His bride, a virgin? Impossible. Confusing. "What about those stories you told me?" As he sat up, cold air prickled across his torso.

Nervously, Amy traced one finger along the edge of the tile. "When we first got to be friends, you assumed I was experienced because I'm older than you. I was too embarrassed to admit I wasn't."

"What about the wrestler who wore your pink sweatshirt? The guy who whisked you off to Tahiti? The men who got down on their knees to propose?"

"Consider them a form of entertainment," Amy said. "I was trying to turn the whole thing into a joke by making the most outrageous claims I could."

"Just now, you knew what you were doing. You can't tell me that was pure instinct." He waited, expecting her to give him a triumphant grin and admit she was kidding.

"It was. Honest." She watched him from beneath her delicate winged eyebrows. "Is it a problem?"

"Not exactly." Quent didn't know why he felt so uncomfortable. Men used to want their brides to be innocent, didn't they? He'd even speculated about it himself. "I wish you'd been straight with me, though."

"I'm sorry." Amy ducked her head. "It never occurred to me, when we started being buddies, that we would reach this point. When you proposed, I figured it didn't matter."

"It doesn't." He wished there was more conviction in his voice.

"I felt as if being a virgin meant that no one wanted me," Amy said.

"That's ridiculous." Where had she come up with that idea? "If the men in Serene Beach weren't pursuing you in droves, they must all have their heads stuck in the ground."

"You'll get no argument from me."

They sat for a while longer, neither of them finding anything to say. Finally Quent got up and turned off the jets. After handing Amy a towel, he wrapped one around his waist.

He remembered one morning at her condo, when he'd run to check on Tara while clutching a towel to his midsection. The casual way Amy had poked fun at him, he'd assumed she'd seen plenty of men in this state or worse. What had really been going through her mind?

A lot of his memories didn't quite click anymore. It was as if he'd married a woman he scarcely knew.

How was that possible? This was Amy, his best friend!

Even after he brushed his teeth and got into the king-size bed, Quent's brain wouldn't stop rehashing the matter. If Amy was a virgin, this marriage was a bigger commitment on her part than he'd understood.

He'd believed they could keep things light. Sure, he knew their relationship would change with time, but only when they were both ready.

What did she expect of him? He didn't want to have that discussion now. Or anytime soon. It bothered him, though, to see her watching him worriedly. Even when he rolled over and faced the other way, Quent could feel Amy's discomfort.

He wanted to offer some reassurance, but he didn't know how. If only they could go back to the way things had been. Fun and games. An easygoing flirtation. Friends who talked readily. Of course, he didn't want to give up being lovers or living together, just to lose this edgy, restless anxiety, as if he'd drawn Amy closer to a void from which he didn't know how to protect her.

They were married and there was no going back. Surely things would work themselves out, Quent thought. With luck, by tomorrow they'd be their old selves again.

He certainly hoped so.

AMY FELT like an idiot.

She of all people should have known better than to get married without revealing her biggest secret. Especially one she'd been lying to Quent about for months.

As a counselor, she also should have realized that she was bound to get hurt if she married a man who didn't return her love. Quent had made it plain that, although he was fond of her, they were tying the knot so they could adopt his niece and nephew.

Knowing him so well, she could guess why he was

withdrawing now. Discovering her virginity had opened his eyes. No woman would wait this long to make love, then give herself to a man, unless she expected him to make her dreams come true.

Despite her independent nature, she had old-fashioned dreams, but maybe Quent didn't. In a sense, Amy had tricked him into becoming her husband when all he wanted was to be a live-in lover and full-time father.

The harm had been done. Now what was she going to do about it?

She nestled deeper into her pillow and stared at Quent's broad, unwelcoming back. What she had to do, she decided, was to keep her end of the bargain.

They'd made an agreement, even if it wasn't explicit. Raise the kids, sleep together and not make emotional demands on each other.

Although it was going to hurt like fire, she had to act like her old self. That was the only way to erase Quent's mistrust.

She had to let go of her dreams, Amy thought, trying to ignore the knot in her stomach. How ironic, that she'd finally gotten everything she wanted, and she felt like bursting into tears.

But she wouldn't. Not, at least, until after Quent fell asleep.

Chapter Fifteen

On Sunday morning, Amy hoped they might make love again. Quent, however, slept late, which wasn't surprising, considering the hard schedule he'd been working. After awakening, he was polite but distracted, and she knew better than to press the issue.

On the drive home, she tried briefly to bring up the subject of their relationship. He got such a strained expression that she didn't pursue the matter.

Soon they reached Serene Beach and were engulfed in the children's welcome and in making plans for the holiday. Amy did her best to act like a carefree companion, and Quent gradually responded. Although it felt strange, as if she were playing a role, it was gratifying to see how much more talkative and cheerful he became.

On Monday, people at work were too busy to notice how hard Amy had to struggle to act normally. Natalie chattered about plans for the yacht party, and Heather wolfed down her lunch and ran out to finish buying her granddaughter's presents.

That night, Quent came home with a Christmas tree. He and Amy decorated it with help from Greg, who handed up the ornaments that Amy's father had sent from his attic. Tara watched and played with a set of wooden animals that had belonged to Quent as a child.

Taking a break from adorning the branches with tinsel, Amy picked up a hand-carved elephant and marveled at its intricate detail. "What's his name?"

"Eddie." Quent fixed the star on the treetop.

"Eddie?"

"Starts with an e for elephant," he said. "It made sense when I was five."

She tried to visualize her husband at that age, but couldn't mentally cram his powerful build into such a tiny package. "How old were you when you decided to become a doctor?"

He adjusted the star and stepped back. "Does that look straight to you?"

"It's crooked," Greg said.

"You're right." Quent fixed it. To Amy, he said, "I must have been a teenager. I used to enjoy watching medical shows on TV. I wanted to save lives the way those doctors did." With a wink, he added, "Besides, they seemed to have a lot of fun."

"Don't they?" she teased.

"Actually, yes," he said. "Don't tell Dr. Fingger or he might assign me more work." After giving the star one last inspection, he nodded his approval. "Done. Now, is anybody in the mood for hot chocolate and marshmallows?"

They all were.

Later, Amy hoped Quent might loosen up and join her in bed, but, before she got up the nerve to ask, he retired to his accustomed couch in her office, as if nothing had changed between them since their wedding. She told herself not to worry. Now that the honeymoon had ended, they needed to build a new relationship day by day.

On Tuesday after dinner, Quent went to his old apartment to pack what belongings he hadn't already taken and to make arrangements to dispose of his meager furnishings. While he was out, Amy baked Christmas cookies, shared them with the children, and put them to bed. Tomorrow night was Christmas Eve, a time for new beginnings.

As she entered the living room, Amy stopped at the sight of the lighted tree. Her attention traveled from the colored bulbs to the glittering ornaments up to the silver star on top. Some gnome figurines she'd bought at the hospital gift shop peered impishly through the branches.

Her mother used to add her own special touches to their Christmas trees. As hard as Amy's father had tried, he'd never been able to duplicate the feat. Or perhaps the holidays had simply never felt the same after she was gone.

She didn't understand how a mother could leave like that. It had been especially hard on Amy, having to deal with adolescence on her own. For a long time, she'd attributed her uncertain sense of femininity and her failure to find the right guy to the lack of a mother's guidance.

Over time, she'd forgiven her mother. Matters weren't perfect between them, though, even now.

After repeatedly failing to reach Frieda by phone, she'd left a message about the wedding. It troubled her that her mother hadn't bothered to respond.

Maybe she was ill. There must be some explanation.

Concerned, Amy went into the kitchen and dialed the number in San Francisco. On the third ring, Frieda answered.

"Are you all right?" Amy said.

"I'm sorry I didn't call back." Her mother sounded wistful. "I knew it would upset your father if I attended, and he deserves better than that. So I stayed away. Congratulations, honey. I hope you're happy."

There was no point in sharing her doubts, so Amy said, "Quent's a terrific man and, as I said in my message, I adore his niece and nephew." When her mother remained silent, she added, "We decorated our tree last night. It reminded me of old times."

"After I left, I always worried about you at Christmas and your birthday," Frieda said. "I should have been there, I know. But I felt trapped. Not your father's fault. I just had to leave."

"Do you still think it was the right decision?"

"Who knows?" Her mother gave a brittle laugh. "Twenty years ago, it was the trendy thing for women my age to leave their family and try to find themselves. At first, it was a tremendously freeing experience. I'd never lived on my own."

"Yet you got married again," Amy pointed out.

"And again and again. Maybe I should have stuck it out the first time." After a pause, her mother said, "Things are going well with Ben. We had some rocky times but that's in the past. His children and grandchildren are joining us for Christmas dinner this year."

"I'm glad to hear it." The last time they'd talked, Frieda hadn't been on speaking terms with her stepchildren. "You're not fighting anymore?"

"Not like we used to."

"What made the difference?"

"I finally accepted that I'm not the center of the known universe and my happiness isn't the only thing that matters. If I'd realized that sooner, I wouldn't have let so many people down," Frieda said. "I don't know that I can make up for it, but I'm trying."

"I love you, Mom." Amy hadn't expected to say the words. They just popped out.

"I love you, too." Had her mother ever told her that before? She couldn't remember. "More than you know. Can you forgive me for what I did?"

"I already have," Amy said.

After they rang off, she was glad she'd called. If anything, the conversation had reinforced her determination to stand by Quent and the children, to make sure they always had her support.

Amy never wanted to look back over the years and reproach herself for letting them down. She knew that, by the time she reached her mother's age, their love and closeness would more than make up for any dreams she sacrificed along the way.

"Boat!" Tara jumped excitedly on the dock. The word was part of her growing vocabulary.

"I wasn't sure she knew that the boat in her bathtub is the same as a boat in the harbor," Quent admitted as he shepherded his family toward the yacht. "I'm glad she made the connection."

The night air invigorated him. He was glad the children had taken naps so they could all enjoy Christmas Eve on the Barr yacht.

"She's a smart child." Amy, wearing a sparkly black jacket over her green dress, held tight to the little girl's hand. Her slim figure and velvety skin made Quent tingle with memories of their lovemaking in the spa. He wanted her again. Maybe tonight. "Like her brother."

Greg gave a happy skip at the compliment and

pointed toward the harbor with a mittened hand. "Look, they've got lights all over the ships. How beautiful!"

"It certainly is." Quent's heart swelled with joy at sharing this experience with his wife and children.

Music and voices drifted toward them as they turned onto the private pier. The yacht, named the *Melissa,* was often used for public relations purposes and staff parties, he'd been told, but this was the first time since his arrival last September that he'd been invited on board.

"Who's Melissa?" he asked Amy. "Patrick's mother?"

"No, his sister," she said. "She died at birth. Patrick's father believed she might have survived if there'd been better medical care, so he devoted the rest of his life to establishing Doctors Circle."

"That's a sad story about the baby," Greg said.

"It has a happy ending," Amy pointed out. "If it weren't for Melissa, lots of other babies might not be alive and well today."

"She must be an angel," the little boy said.

"I'm sure she is."

Quent wondered how Amy managed to say exactly the right thing at the right time to the children. She had a talent for relating to people. It felt good being around her, yet he missed the emotional closeness they'd shared the evening of their honeymoon.

Although they talked and joked easily again, something was still missing. He hoped they'd get back to normal soon.

Ahead, Patrick and Natalie waved to them from the deck. "Come on up!" called their host. "Need any help?"

"You can grab these little guys." Quent lifted each child in turn, and Patrick caught them seamlessly.

Amy, hindered by her dress, hesitated as she eyed the short gap between pier and deck. Gripping her waist with both hands, Quent eased her across. Through the thin fabric, he felt her body's vibrancy. Awareness pulsated through him, all the way to his fingertips.

He wished he weren't on call tonight. With luck, however, they'd still find time to be alone together and perhaps recapture their intimacy.

After Quent leaped on board, Patrick pumped his hand. "Glad you could come."

"This is an impressive setup." Quent gestured at the yacht's sleek lines illuminated by a wealth of white lights. There was even an electrical Christmas tree atop the cabin, blinking red and green.

"The food and drinks are inside," Natalie told him.

"Including the nonalcoholic variety," her husband added jovially. "We don't want anyone tumbling over the railings."

"I may have to work later, so no eggnog for me," Quent said.

Amy's mouth twisted. "I almost forgot about your being on call." Apparently their physical connection had stirred her, too.

"Isn't there a rule that nobody's allowed to give birth at Doctors Circle on Christmas Eve?" He winked. "Don't they prefer to wait for New Year's Eve so they can have a crack at the 'first baby of the year' prize?"

"I hope so." Amy ventured a smile. It suited her so well, he resolved to make her smile as often as possible tonight.

As more guests arrived and claimed their hosts' attention, the young family wandered along the railing.

The children exclaimed over every detail of the boat, and other partygoers kept up a stream of greetings and good wishes on their marriage.

Around the harbor, houses blazed gloriously. From inside the boat drifted Christmas music. Amy, her face bright from the chill air, slipped her hand into Quent's. It felt warm and welcoming.

This was going to be a night to remember, he thought.

With a stiff breeze blowing off the water, the air was growing chilly, so they went inside. Tantalizing aromas washed over them as they entered the spacious main room. Couches lined the walls and long tables offered a wealth of food. Since the yacht wasn't sailing tonight, there was no need to worry about rough seas.

Heather called hello, and they both responded in kind. She stood by the buffet table, helping herself to hors d'oeuvres while chatting with the head of the radiology department. There was no sign of her daughter or granddaughter.

"Is she still keeping certain matters private?" Quent was careful not to mention any details because, in this crowd, there might be attentive ears.

"Yes. She's determined to avoid being the subject of office gossip, and I'm glad she's succeeding." Amy scanned the room. "Do you see Mrs. McLanahan? I'd like to wish her Merry Christmas."

Miriam James, the manager of the Birthing Center's gift shop, stopped on her way past them. "I couldn't help overhearing," she said. "Can you believe it, Noreen insisted on keeping the gift shop open this evening."

"She ought to be enjoying the party," Amy said. "Is she coming later?"

"I told her to close as early as she can, but she said she intended to stick around in case people want to buy last-minute presents and flowers." The young woman shook her head. "That woman is a saint. I sure love her."

"We all do," Amy said.

Tara wriggled in Quent's arms. "Hungry," she said.

"That's two syllables!" It was only the second or third time he'd heard his niece use such a big word. "An important step in her development."

"A true breakthrough." Amy grinned.

"She's adorable!" Miriam might have said more, but someone was gesturing to her. She excused herself and moved off.

"I'm hungry, too," Greg said.

"Let's eat." At the buffet, Quent supervised his nephew and Amy filled a plate for Tara. He would have liked to sit with the two of them but Greg was too energized to hold still. "If it's okay with you, we'll nibble while we circulate."

"Go ahead," Amy said. "We'll be fine."

He made sure she and Tara were settled before he allowed Greg to pull him away. The little boy was particularly interested in inspecting the other children. In the past, Quent had never paid much attention to youngsters at this kind of event, but now he took pleasure in observing their interaction with their parents and with Greg. The world was a different place since he had kids of his own.

From time to time, he found himself the object of attention from staffers. Nurse Sue Anne, noticing that an overhead wreath was made of mistletoe, planted a kiss on Quent's cheek, and Hallie, the receptionist from the Well-Baby Clinic, gushed about how cute Greg was without taking her eyes off Quent. Well, he used to enjoy flirting at parties, so how could he blame them?

He'd like to get Amy under the mistletoe and claim a kiss from his new bride. Quent's desire for her didn't abate even when they were on opposite sides of the room.

It annoyed him that men kept looking at her with interest that, thank goodness, she showed no sign of returning. Still, it was a relief when Hallie engaged her in conversation, effectively keeping everyone else at bay.

Quent checked his watch. It was too early to leave yet, he supposed. Silently, he willed the pregnant women of Serene Beach to refrain from having any difficult deliveries on Christmas Eve.

Greg tugged his hand, wanting to go outside again. Quent decided to start teaching him the names of the constellations. It would be fun for them both, and it would help the time pass quickly.

"THIS BABY is so sweet!" Hallie cooed. She was an attractive young woman with long chestnut hair and hazel eyes. "I don't blame you for marrying Quent so he could keep these little darlings. Of course, if it were me, I'd make sure things didn't stay platonic."

"Now, there's an idea." Amy couldn't resist a touch of irony.

"Not that I'm complaining," the receptionist dithered on. "I don't mind his having a marriage of convenience with you as long as he's still available to the rest of us."

"Is that what he told you?" Into Amy's mind flashed an image of Quent from a few weeks ago, leaning on the counter at the Well-Baby Clinic gazing at this same woman.

"Well, sure, I guess." Hallie gave a small pout. "I mean, everybody knows it."

Even though she knew that was the rumor circulating at the clinic, Amy cringed. She hated the way women kept treating Quent as if he were still single. The worst part was the suspicion that he might be encouraging them.

A feedback screech from a microphone hushed the chatter. Clamping her hands to her ears, Hallie retreated.

"Sorry about that," Patrick said from the front of the room, where he stood with a mike in one hand. "I'm trying to make an announcement."

"I hope it's 'Merry Christmas!'" someone called.

"Let's start there," said the center's administrator. "Merry Christmas, everybody."

Shouts of "Merry Christmas!" flew back at him. People drifted in from outside, including Quent. Amy was glad to see there weren't any women hanging on him this time.

"This isn't a formal announcement, but we're a family here and we share things." Tall and self-assured, Patrick was at home in front of a crowd. "I want you all to be the first to know that, with the help of my brother-in-law Mike Lincoln, we've secured a major pledge for the Endowment Fund."

Applause broke out. "How much?" a man called.

"I'm not at liberty to say." He paused, giving the guests a chance to make vocal protests along the lines of, "I thought we shared things!" and "You can't hold out on us!" Patrick feigned dismay. "You mean, you want me to tell you now?"

Natalie, glowing with goodwill, watched her husband

play with the crowd. The two of them were a perfect match, both devoted to the medical center and to each other. And, of course, to their child-to-be.

"Put us out of our misery!" Heather called.

"Well, if you insist," Patrick said. "I really can't reveal the name of the company yet, but I can tell you that we've been pledged ten million dollars in matching funds."

Whoops and cheers rocked the yacht. Since an equivalent amount had already been raised, the center was two-thirds of the way to reaching its goal.

With that much money, Doctors Circle would be on solid financial footing for years to come. Under Patrick's guidance, it had recovered from a former administrator's incompetence enough to permit the current remodeling. Thanks to the new donations, there should be plenty of funds for the future as well.

"The tricky part is the word *matching*," Patrick said when the hubbub abated. "The community has to come up with an equivalent amount. Think we can encourage them to do that?"

A chorus of yeses filled the air. Amy joined in, and so did Tara.

"Yes! Yes!" the little girl continued shouting after everyone else stopped, to the crowd's amusement.

Patrick raised a glass. "Here's to our ardent young supporter. May Doctors Circle be here for her and every other little girl in this community when they grow up!"

Applause broke out. Through the crowd, Amy's gaze met Quent's. He was grinning, and she knew she was, too.

They broke contact as a pretty young woman moved in front of him, blocking Amy's view. She recognized the newcomer as a cafeteria worker who'd loaded up

Quent's plate extra high once as the two of them went through the line. Although she couldn't hear what the woman was saying, there was no mistaking her intent as she tugged him under the wreath and planted a kiss on his mouth.

Reddening, Quent ducked away. Despite his embarrassment, it appeared to Amy that he enjoyed the game.

He couldn't help the fact that females found him attractive. She wished he weren't quite so entertained by it, though.

NORMALLY, Quent hated leaving a party in full swing. This time, he was glad that the yawning kids gave him an excuse. Although ten o'clock, the hour when he went on call, was fast approaching, he hoped to have some uninterrupted time with Amy.

They sang carols on the way to the condo. Greg didn't know the words but gamely hummed along, while Tara babbled merrily.

Amy's sweet soprano sent tingles up Quent's spine as he drove through the quiet streets of Serene Beach. There was something bewitching about singing these beautiful songs in the star-flung night.

As they passed between arrays of Christmas lights on the houses, he imagined them as characters on a sleigh dashing across a wintry landscape inside a paperweight his mother used to own. The main difference was that, even if you shook southern California and held it upside down, you wouldn't get any snow.

Amy leaned back, singing the words to "Feliz Navidad" with gusto. Quent had been right. Matters had fallen into place. He felt as if nothing had ever come between them.

At home, he carried a half-asleep Tara inside. Amy

took charge of Greg, who was insisting on a bath. It seemed easier to give in than to fight, so the two of them disappeared into the bathroom.

This time, when Quent changed his niece's diaper, he had no trouble tightening it the proper amount. The skill hadn't taken more than a few days to become second nature.

"You're getting me trained," he told Tara.

"Train," she said. "Choo choo!"

Quent laughed. "Not that kind of train. But hey, you never know. Maybe my little girl will grow up to be an engineer."

Or whatever she wanted to be. A doctor, a psychologist, a teacher, a homemaker. She was going to be the mistress of her own destiny, with Quent and Amy right behind her, lending support.

Warmly dressed in a sleeper, the baby chatted to him on the way to her crib. After laying her down on her back, Quent stood watching for a few minutes until she drifted into sleep.

On the nearby bureau, a couple of teddy bears sat watching them. Childhood buddies were the best kind, he thought.

When he tore himself away, he went to check on Amy and Greg. From outside the bathroom, he could hear the gurgle of the drain emptying, along with the buffing sound of a towel being employed.

Inside, Greg was talking. Quent didn't want to interrupt, so he waited.

"Can I call you Mommy?" the little boy said.

"I'd love it." More rubbing sounds. "Did you have fun tonight?"

"Kind of."

"Just 'kind of'?" Amy sounded surprised. "I thought you liked the boat."

"I did. The food, too."

"Was there something you didn't like?"

"Well…" The word vanished into a yawn.

"Here, I brought you some new pajamas," Amy said. "What do you think?"

"I like the elves." Apparently, he was referring to pictures on the fabric. There was a pause while, Quent assumed, arms fitted into sleeves and pants got pulled on.

He wished they'd get back to the part about what Greg didn't like. The loud music, maybe? Or was it being near water?

The boy hadn't shown any fear of water despite the trauma of the accident, Lucy had reported. Until now, it hadn't occurred to Quent that being on a boat might affect his nephew.

But he doubted that was the issue. Greg had leaned over the railing at one point, fearlessly pointing out a ripple that he insisted was a dolphin. So what else could be bothering him?

It was a relief to hear Amy say, "Now tell me what you didn't like tonight."

"Why did those ladies kiss Uncle Quent?" Greg replied.

"You mean under the mistletoe?" Amy asked. "It's kind of a tradition."

Quent hadn't realized she'd noticed those incidents. Or that Greg had, either.

"I don't like it," said his nephew. "He's married to you."

"They were just being friendly. Quent's such a handsome man that lots of women like him." When Amy spoke again, her tone had altered. "No, I'm not being completely honest, and I always want to tell you the truth, because you're my son."

"Okay," Greg said.

Quent had to remind himself to breathe. He didn't know why he'd suddenly grown tense.

"Getting married means we're going to be your parents," she said. "Forever and ever."

"Good!"

"But people get married for different reasons, and the other ladies know that," she said.

"People get married for love," Greg said. "Lucy told me."

"Yes, but sometimes one person loves the other one more." Amy's voice trembled. "Your uncle Quent made a sacrifice and married his friend so we could give you and Tara a good home. And I'm glad he did, because you know what? I love him a whole bunch."

Stunned, Quent moved away from the door. Amy loved him. She didn't mean as a friend, either. And she was hurting, hurting deeply, because he didn't respond in kind.

He didn't know what to do. He'd believed he was marrying an experienced, devil-may-care woman. Instead, his wife had turned out to be a virgin who genuinely loved him and who, apparently, wanted a traditional marriage. Although he cared about her deeply, he wasn't sure he could give her that.

Even a guy like him, who wasn't always lightning fast when it came to noticing a woman's emotions, could tell how much pain he was causing Amy. Had this arrangement been a mistake? The last thing he wanted was to go through life disappointing her. But what choice did he have?

His eyes smarted. It must be the late hour, Quent decided, and went into the kitchen to remove his contact lenses.

He was cleaning his glasses when the phone rang. A glance at his watch showed it to be 10:11 p.m. So it came as no surprise when the charge nurse said into his ear, "Dr. Ladd? You're needed in labor and delivery."

"I'll be there in fifteen minutes."

In the hallway, he informed Amy of the call and gave Greg a good-night hug. After assuring them that he'd return as soon as his work was done, Quent threw on a coat and went out.

He pretended not to notice the uncertainty on his wife's face. Although his instincts urged him to reassure her that he couldn't wait to get back to her, he needed to be as honest with her as she'd been with Greg.

A few hours of hard work ought to help him sort out his thoughts, he mused as he got in his vehicle. But one thing was clear.

There was no way they could go back to what he'd considered normality, now that he knew how Amy really felt.

Chapter Sixteen

At forty-one, the mother was having her first baby, not an unusual occurrence in these days of high-power careers and postponed childbearing. She'd run into a problem at the end and Rob Sentinel had performed an emergency Caesarian section.

As soon as the baby was handed to him, Quent tuned out everyone else in the operating room and focused on checking the infant's responses. There'd been a brief period when oxygen might have been cut off, and he hoped there'd been no damage.

The newest resident of Serene Beach had a shock of dark hair, a chubby body and a rosebud mouth. His heart sounded fine. Breathing was normal. Reflexes checked out. Everything looked great.

Quent gazed down into a pair of inquisitive blue eyes. "You're going to be fine," he told the tiny boy, and handed him to a nurse to be diapered, wrapped and placed beside his mother.

Not until he left the room and stripped off his soiled gloves and clothing did Quent realize how fast his heart was beating. He'd been concerned for that baby in a deeply personal way.

It was because he knew what it meant to love a child with all his heart. Two children, in fact.

At some level, he'd always recognized that his job brought him in contact with miracles. Tonight, though, he understood more completely than ever what was at stake. A future full of promise now stretched ahead of this little guy, thanks to his parents, Doctors Circle and a dose of good luck.

A miracle on Christmas Eve. What more could a man ask for?

After washing his hands, Quent scribbled his notes for the medical chart. He was nearly done when Rob joined him. "Everything okay?" the obstetrician asked.

"Thank goodness, yes," Quent said. "I don't see any problems."

"I'll let the father know. He'll be thrilled. They've waited a long time for this child." The mother, now sedated and on her way to the recovery room, would be too woozy to absorb the information for a while, Quent knew.

His friend began cleaning up. In profile, Rob was a handsome man, with dark hair and classic features. Also a recent arrival in Serene Beach, he hadn't yet found a girlfriend. Thank goodness the date with Amy hadn't amounted to anything.

Quent smiled, realizing that he himself had managed to find not only a girlfriend but a wife and two kids. Quite an accomplishment for a guy whose idea of commitment only a few months ago had been paying cash for a used Ping-Pong table.

"It doesn't seem fair that you have to work tonight." Rob tossed his white coat into the soiled-clothing container. "Being a newlywed and all."

"I owed Dudley a favor." Quent shrugged. "Besides, we all have to take our share of holiday hours."

"Want a word of advice from a guy who used to be married?" Rob said. "Don't leave your wife alone any more than you have to."

"I didn't realize you were divorced." It wasn't the kind of topic men usually discussed. Quent knew which football team Rob rooted for and that he preferred imported beer. Until recently, those had seemed like the most important details. "Any kids?"

A tight shake of the head was the response. Sore subject, Quent gathered. "Think you'll be needing me again tonight?"

"There's no one else in labor," Rob said. "Of course, it's possible women are delaying coming in so they can enjoy the festivities, in which case we may get an influx later. I think I'll sleep over." He could use an unoccupied bed, of which there were plenty due to the lack of elective surgeries on a holiday.

Quent thought about the cheery condo that awaited him, with lights blazing, a wreath over the door and cookies in the kitchen. Rob probably had nothing in his apartment to go home to.

He wondered what had gone wrong in the man's marriage. Perhaps the long hours involved in medical training had proved fatal. That wasn't unusual. Doctors, like police officers, had a high divorce rate.

"By the way," Rob said, "you got some goop on your glasses. You might want to clean that off before you drive home."

"Gee, I thought the lights were kind of dim in here. Thanks. Merry Christmas." Quent was cleaning his spectacles for the second time that evening as his friend departed.

If Amy was awake, they could enjoy the glimmering tree together, he thought. As for making love later, he was no longer sure how to proceed.

Discovering she was a virgin had forced him to face how little he knew her. Since their honeymoon, he'd begun to believe everything was back to normal. What he'd heard tonight, however, made Quent realize she must have been putting on a cheerful front for his benefit.

Lost in thought, he notified the charge nurse that he was leaving, and headed into a side corridor. As he approached the staff entrance, Amy's words to Greg echoed through his mind.

Sometimes one person loves the other one more. Your uncle Quent made a sacrifice...

She'd declared her love for him in a way that left no doubt he was breaking her heart. Although a four-year-old boy might not understand, Quent did.

He halted just inside the door. Next Christmas, would his wife still be here? Why should she stick with a husband who didn't love her the way she deserved? Rob's wife obviously hadn't.

A bleak vista appeared in Quent's mind. A cold, cheerless apartment. A hired caretaker watching the children. A series of casual dates with women who vanished from his thoughts the moment they disappeared from sight.

Why hadn't he realized at their wedding that Amy loved him? He'd noticed the radiance that surrounded her. He must have guessed the truth, yet he'd refused to admit it to himself. Why?

Because love terrifies me.

The words came out of nowhere. They startled Quent into turning and pacing away from the exit. His footsteps carried him at random while long-suppressed feelings erupted to the surface.

Since that night on the quay when the railing collapsed, he'd experienced anxiety whenever he and Amy became close. An unidentified danger had seemed to surround him, retreating only when he pulled back from the relationship.

Vaguely, he'd realized it had something to do with his family experiences. He'd assumed he wanted to avoid ending up like his parents, whose marriage had deteriorated into barely disguised hostility.

He'd believed his concern was protecting his friendship with Amy. But that wasn't true. The person he'd been trying to protect was himself.

Quent paused at the edge of the empty lobby, where a Christmas tree blinked forlornly. With a jolt, he saw another waiting room from a little over a year ago, heard the murmur of low voices and smelled its antiseptic scent as if he'd been transported.

That night in San Diego, he'd rushed to his father's side after receiving the phone call. Even amid the bustling life of the hospital, there'd been no hope left for his mother, Jeffrey or Paula. By the time Quent arrived, all that remained was the agonizing business of signing forms and making funeral arrangements.

Gone, so quickly. So absolutely. For all his medical training, Quent had been helpless.

What if someday it happened to Amy? What if he let himself love her, heart and soul, and had to stand in a room like this and learn that she was gone?

It didn't seem so unlikely, not after she'd nearly been injured twice in his company. The memory made his eyes burn.

He hadn't dared to love her, because he might lose

her. And if that happened, he didn't know how he would survive.

At the far side of the lobby, he heard the scrape of a door. Dragged from his reflections, Quent saw Mrs. McLanahan turn to lock the gift shop.

She'd stayed outrageously late, he thought. Maybe the widow had found dusting the shelves and double-checking the receipts preferable to spending the evening in an empty house.

Glad for a respite from his troubling reflections, he called a greeting and crossed the lobby. At least he could walk the elderly woman to her car and wish her a Merry Christmas.

Then he'd go home himself. He only wished he knew what he was going to say when he got there.

AMY AWOKE from a dream in which a Grinch stole her pancake mix and she was trying to get the children to eat bagels with syrup on them. That, she thought as her eyes blinked open, must be the stupidest dream anyone ever had on Christmas morning.

Last night, she'd waited up for an hour after Quent left, bringing wrapped gifts out of the closet and arranging them under the tree. She'd also mixed pancake batter and made orange juice for this morning's special breakfast.

She'd hoped he would come home in time for them to enjoy a late-night cup of cocoa together. Weariness had overcome her good intentions, however.

It was too bad none of the extended family had accepted their invitation to dinner, Amy mused as she showered. After traveling to Serene Beach for the wedding only last Saturday, the others had decided against making the trip again so soon. Even Lucy was too busy, although she'd promised to visit before she left for Kansas City.

Although Amy would miss everyone, she didn't regret the chance to spend the day alone with her family. Still, having other people around might make it easier to pretend there were no problems.

She'd done her best to keep Quent from guessing how much it upset her to see other women flirting with him. It wouldn't get easier when they went back to work tomorrow, either. Amy wasn't sure she could rein in her temper if Hallie made any more remarks about how *she* would never maintain a platonic marriage to Quent.

"You asked for it," she told herself. "So quit complaining."

After her shower, she dried her hair and dressed in jeans and a festive sweater. When she emerged, she noted that Quent's door was shut. Until now, she hadn't even been certain he'd come home last night.

Greg poked his head out of the children's room. "Did Santa come?" he asked eagerly. "Can I go see?"

It was on the tip of Amy's tongue to agree when she realized that Quent wouldn't want to miss such a special occasion with the children. "Let's see if your uncle's awake," she said.

"I can't wait!" Greg hopped from one foot to another. He looked adorable in his new pajamas with elves appliquéd on the front.

Surely Quent would forgive her for waking him, Amy thought. "I'll get him up."

"Okay. Hurry!"

She tapped on the office door. If only the two of them shared a room, she'd have known what time he came home and he'd probably have awakened when she did. No doubt they'd get into a rhythm eventually.

Amy was about to try the knob when Quent opened the door himself. He looked remarkably bright-eyed behind his glasses. "You didn't start without me, did you?" he asked, tightening the belt on his robe. With his hair rumpled and his pajama collar creased, he radiated the playful air she loved.

"No, of course not." Her spirits rose. For one thing, he wasn't avoiding her gaze this morning. For another, judging by his expression, he was almost as excited as his nephew. "Tara's not up."

"She doesn't know about Santa yet," Greg said.

"Well, she's going to learn," Quent said. "Since this is our first Christmas as a family, let's establish some traditions."

"Like what?" asked the boy.

"Here's the first one." He swept Amy into a hug, then planted a kiss on her mouth. Although it wasn't the slow, sexy kind, it felt wonderful.

"I like that tradition." Reluctantly, she released her grip on his shoulders. The scent of his hair clung to her.

"Here's the second part." He lifted Greg so high the boy could touch the ceiling. "Okay, we've established that you can fly. How are you at landings?"

Greg giggled. "Not too fast!"

Carefully, Quent lowered him. "One elf, coming down to earth."

"Do it again!"

"Okay. In the meantime, I hope Amy will be kind enough to get Tara. Because the third part of the tradition is that we all go together to see what Santa brought."

"I'd be happy to." Quent's mood made him irresistible, and Amy intended to enjoy every minute of the day. This was as close to heaven as she had any right to expect.

Within minutes, they were all assembled in the hallway. Although Tara had no idea what was going on, she mirrored their anticipation.

"Let's not start shouting if we find a big guy in a red coat sleeping off his busy night," Quent said. "We'll just quietly take whatever's left in his bag of toys, okay?"

"Santa won't be asleep!" Greg chortled. "He's back at the North Pole."

"Quent, I can't believe you're proposing to mug Santa!" Amy added in mock reproof.

"Finders keepers." He winked at her. "Okay, let's go!"

As they surged forward, Amy hoped Quent wouldn't mind that this year, with so much going on, she hadn't been very imaginative in buying things for him. She doubted he'd even remembered to get her a gift. That was okay with her. Christmas was for the children.

When Greg reached the pile of presents beneath the tree, he gave a shout. "Look! Santa put our pictures on them so we know who gets what!"

"That was clever," Quent said under his breath.

"I was picking up a roll of film and it occurred to me I could make good use of the pictures, since the kids can't read yet," she explained in a low voice. Last night, she'd piled each child's gifts separately, with a photo on top. As a lark, she'd done the same with Quent's gifts.

To her surprise, she saw three large wrapped boxes that hadn't been there when she went to bed. Instead of a photo, they were topped by a stick-figure drawing of a woman done on a sheet from a medical prescription pad. "Now, who could have left this?"

"Santa must have consulted one of his medical elves," Quent said.

Greg was already tearing the paper off his largest box. "Here are the rules!" Quent announced. "Each person gets to open one present. Then the next person, and so on. We keep going around until we're done."

"Who made those rules?" Although Amy liked the idea, she didn't want her new husband to set himself up as domestic lawgiver. "At our house, it was every man for himself."

"It's an old Ladd tradition," he said.

"Mom and Dad did it that way, too." Greg, having elected himself to go first, yanked off a large bow. With a cry of delight, his little sister grabbed it and sat down to play with what was, for her, apparently the best toy of all.

Amy sat on the couch and watched Quent help his nephew open the large set of Lego pieces. "You can play with it after breakfast," she said. "Don't forget, we're keeping them in my room so Tara won't eat them."

"Okay!" Getting into the spirit of the day, Greg turned to his sister. "Do you want me to help you open your present?"

"Open!" she said. The top package revealed a set of rubber bath duckies. Still hanging on to the bow, Tara gathered them to her. "Bath!"

"We'll do that later, honey," Amy said. "Quent, you're next."

"Nope." Sitting on the floor, he wrapped his arms around his knees. "You start."

Although she was dying of curiosity, she said, "I thought the pattern was boy-girl-boy-girl."

"Fooled you," he said. "It's older child, then younger child, then older adult, younger adult."

"I have to go start the coffee." In the excitement, she'd forgotten. "Go ahead." Hurrying out of the room, Amy smiled to herself. If Quent figured himself to be the boss of this household, he had another think coming.

By the time she returned, he'd given in to temptation and was smoothing out a sweatshirt and sweatpants with the name of his favorite baseball team on them. "All right! Go team!"

"Go! Team!" echoed Tara.

"Your turn, Mommy," said Greg.

The name sent a happy shiver through Amy. "What can this be?" She hefted the top package, which felt as if it might contain clothing.

"Open it!" Greg said.

Inside, Amy found a hand-painted silk nightgown and peignoir. "This is gorgeous." The colors suited her perfectly, and she knew how sensual it would feel next to her skin. "Thank you, Santa!"

"Why are you looking at Daddy?" Greg didn't seem to notice that he'd applied the name to his uncle. She saw a flare of recognition on Quent's face, however.

"Because he put in a good word for me," she said. "Somebody had to let Santa know that I haven't been naughty this year."

"Not nearly naughty enough," Quent murmured. Fortunately, Greg was too busy opening his next gift to pay any attention.

He cheered when he saw that it contained a prereading computer game with his favorite cartoon characters. Tara liked her next present, a teddy bear, so much that she dropped the bow to hug it. For Quent, there was a new hardcover novel by his favorite science-fiction author, which he tucked away to read later.

Curious, Amy lifted her second box, which weighed even less than the first. "I can't imagine how Santa found anything so light," she said. "He must have been worried about the weight limit on his sleigh."

"Quit trying to second-guess Saint Nick and open it," said her husband.

Lying on a nest of tissue paper, Amy found a generous gift certificate to her favorite shoe store. "This is great!" With a twinkle, she added, "Santa must have heard that a certain person forgot to pack my shoes."

Greg snatched up his third gift. "My turn!" After tearing off the wrappings, he found a collection of sand toys that Lucy had sent. "Can we go to the beach?"

"We'll go Saturday, if the weather's good," Amy said. Although the water would be too cold for swimming, the beach should be pleasant if the sun came out.

"I'll help you build a castle," Quent promised.

Inside her package, Tara was thrilled to find sand toys of her own. For himself, Quent unwrapped an umbrella and coordinated hat. "I see somebody noticed I don't own much rain gear."

"Mommy has an umbrella," Greg pointed out.

"Yes, but it won't cover all four of us," Amy said. "I'm sorry I—I mean, Santa—didn't come up with anything more clever. He had short notice."

"That's okay. Your last present is kind of small." Quent indicated the box, which was every bit as large as the other two.

"Mostly tissue paper?" Amy guessed.

"Something like that. Santa ran out of time." To

Greg, he explained, "The elves leave the grown-ups for last."

"Let's see what's inside!" Greg said.

Amy discovered that she didn't want to open it. Not right away. She'd purposely given Quent impersonal presents, because anything more intimate might make him uncomfortable. He'd been more imaginative with his choices, such as the nightgown set, but Amy wanted more, so much more. She ached for her husband to love her the way she loved him. She wanted him to show that this marriage of convenience had a chance of becoming a real union of two souls.

There was no way his last gift could accomplish that. If she opened the package now, the disappointment would show on her face. Her fervent attempts to maintain the fiction that everything was fine would be ruined, along with the rest of the day.

"You know what?" she said. "I'm starving. I'll bet you guys are, too. Let's eat and I'll save this for later when we're not so rushed."

"You promised pancakes." Needing no urging, Greg started for the kitchen.

"Then pancakes it shall be."

"Cakes!" echoed Tara.

Quent's jaw twitched as if he meant to object. When the little girl scampered in her brother's wake, however, he shrugged. "Maybe it is a good idea to wait until later."

"Great."

Soon the pancakes were sizzling on the electric grill while Quent poured orange juice. Tara, who no longer spilled much, took pride in drinking out of her sipper cup.

The rest of the morning passed in a blur. It was fun

helping the children play with their new toys, and there were phone calls to make to the grandparents and Lucy. Amy managed to delay opening her last gift.

She hoped that, once the children lay down for their naps, she and Quent could snatch some time alone. She didn't torment herself with the vain hope that anything had changed. She simply wanted to be with him, even if they were playing a video game or reading books side by side.

Although the unopened present teased at her mind, she was still feeling vulnerable. Better to wait until it didn't seem like a big deal.

After lunch, Amy put Tara to bed and read to Greg. He dozed off halfway through the book.

The condo had fallen silent by the time Amy came out to look for Quent. She found him in the office, fully dressed and sound asleep on his folded-out couch.

He'd worked late last night. No wonder he was tired, Amy told herself, trying to ignore her letdown. This was a great Christmas. The best ever. She didn't want to mar it by wishing for things she couldn't have.

In the kitchen, she poured herself a cup of coffee and set out a leftover muffin from lunch. As she finished the snack, it struck her that it might be wise to open her third present alone. That way, when it turned out to be another gift certificate or a joke item, she could prepare a credible expression of pleasure before her husband awoke. Pleased at the idea, she carried her cup and plate to the sink.

In the living room, toys spilled across the floor. Quent's new jogging outfit lay draped over the back of the couch alongside Amy's peignoir. How much this room had changed in the six weeks since she'd invited him back after their jog, she thought, and not merely because of the storm repairs, either.

Before, everything had been orderly and under control. And lonely, although she hadn't admitted it to herself. Now it vibrated with messy, energetic life.

Smiling, Amy sat down on the sofa. She was finally in the mood to open her last gift.

Chapter Seventeen

As Amy had suspected, most of the contents were tissue paper. What she didn't expect was the long jeweler's box ensconced in the center.

Her heartbeat speeded. Almost afraid to open it, she rubbed her fingers over the velvety surface. *Please don't let this be Quent's idea of a joke.* Scarcely daring to breathe, she pried the edges apart.

A curve of diamonds sparkled at her. Amy drew in a sharp breath. She remembered trying not to stare at the necklace when she and Quent visited the jewelry store. What she loved most was that the delicate design matched the one on her wedding ring.

As she picked it up, the diamonds blazed with brilliant clarity. When and why had Quent purchased it? Surely he hadn't secretly bought the necklace before their wedding and saved it until Christmas, she thought. Only a man deeply in love would do that.

As she fastened it around her neck, Amy spotted a card tucked inside the jeweler's box. Her fingers suddenly clumsy, she fumbled twice before managing to extract it.

As she read silently, a masculine voice from the hallway spoke the words aloud. Quent seemed to be inside her head as he voiced what he'd written in the note. "I love you and I'm glad we're married."

Amy couldn't move. This had to be a fantasy. She didn't want to turn around and break the spell.

"I hope you like it." Quent crossed toward her. "If not, we can exchange it for something else."

Amy's fingers tightened on the card. "How—why—?"

"Can you forgive me for being such an oaf?" A woman could get lost in those sea-blue eyes, so close to hers, she reflected as he sat beside her. "It took me a long time to understand why I held back. I was afraid, Amy."

She could hardly swallow. "Of what?"

"In one night, I lost three people I loved. I became a doctor so I could save people, and then I was utterly powerless to help them." She'd never seen such vulnerability on Quent's face. "Twice, you were nearly injured, right in my arms. I could lose you, too."

"Life doesn't offer insurance policies. We have to take our chances." Amy curved her palm around his cheek and felt the suppleness beneath the morning stubble.

"What I felt wasn't logical." He lowered his hand onto hers. "I didn't even know what was going on inside me. The way I grew up, we never talked about our troubles. We avoided them and hoped they'd go away."

Although Amy wanted to grab the man and kiss him senseless, she needed answers first. "What changed your mind?"

"Last night, I heard you talking to Greg and realized how much harm I was doing by keeping you at arm's length." Quent's gaze seared into hers. "Then at the hospital, the memories of losing my family hit me like a slug in the jaw. That's when I saw that I'd been afraid to love because life is so fragile. But you know what? I can't help it. I fell in love with you anyway.''

"I love you no matter what lies ahead," Amy said. "I'll take whatever time we're given, and treasure every second of it."

A smile started at one corner of his mouth and spread until his whole face glowed. "Does this mean I'm forgiven for acting like a jerk?"

"On one condition," Amy said.

"What's that?"

"You repeat the part where you say you love me."

Strong arms pulled her onto Quent's lap and he buried his face in her hair. "I love you, I will always love you, and I'd marry you again a thousand times if I got the chance."

"You're not still angry because I didn't tell you the truth about being a virgin?"

"Hey, I'm the master at avoiding important issues," he said. "How can I blame you for doing the same?"

"Kiss me, you big lug, and make me forget everything except..." His mouth came down on hers, cutting off the words. Time stood still, and it would have suited Amy fine if it never moved again.

When he came up for air, Quent said, "Any more questions?"

"No. I mean, yes."

"Fire away."

"How did you get the necklace?"

He chuckled. "You can thank Mrs. McLanahan for that. Right after my big revelation, while I was walking her to her car, I wished out loud that it wasn't too late to buy this for you."

"So she waved her fairy godmother wand and it appeared in the parking garage?" Amy teased.

"The jeweler is her friend, remember?" he said. "She persuaded the poor guy to come down to his store in the middle of the night and sell me the necklace."

"On Christmas Eve?" Amy couldn't believe anyone was that good-hearted.

"Apparently he's a lonely widower who was sitting up watching a rerun of *It's a Wonderful Life*. I believe an invitation to brunch today also featured into the bargain." Quent shook his head in amazement. "We owe that woman a great deal."

"She's a sweetheart. I hope she enjoys her brunch," Amy said.

"So do I." To her surprise, he struggled to his feet while still holding her. Amazingly, he only staggered a little. "Time to carry my bride across the threshold."

"We already did that."

"Hotel rooms don't count," Quent said.

"You're not going outside in your bathrobe!" She giggled at the thought.

"I had a different threshold in mind," said her husband.

She understood perfectly a minute later when they crossed into Amy's bedroom and closed the door behind them.

THE JANUARY SKY darkened early over the ocean. On the beach, coals glowed in the barbecue pits and the scent of roasting chickens drifted through the salty air.

"Time to wash up," Amy told the children, although the best she would be able to do with premoistened towels was to scrub their faces and hands. Sand clung to their feet and legs, drifted through the folds of their clothing and even, she suspected, infiltrated their hair. "Oh, dear. I'm barely going to make a dent."

"What's a beach party without sand in the food?" asked Natalie, setting out picnic supplies by the light of a hurricane lamp.

"Let's see how long your laissez-faire attitude holds up once you give birth." Heather removed containers of potato salad and coleslaw from a cooler, although the night air was growing so nippy that the food hadn't needed chilling.

After glancing around to make sure none of their other friends could overhear, Amy said, "You're not too old to give birth again yourself, you know."

"Don't mention it! It's a jinx!" Heather cried in mock horror. "I'd need a husband, which I assure you I don't remotely want."

"I'll take your word for it," Amy said.

In the fading light, she had trouble checking the children's faces and hands for stubborn dirt. "Quent!" she called. "If you want them operating-room clean, you're going to have to finish the job yourself."

Her husband waved from beside the barbecue, where he, Patrick and Rob were moving chicken and steaks onto platters. He cupped his hand to his ear to indicate he'd missed most of what she said, no doubt thanks to the rumble of the surf. Amy waved to indicate it didn't matter.

"Clueless," Heather said. "Like most guys. Of course, he's cute, which makes up for a lot."

"Your tongue is sharp tonight." Amy released the children, who scampered across the beach to their father. "What gives?"

"My daughter tells me her fiancé's returning from overseas duty in March," Heather said. "She and Ginger will move out as soon as he finds a place. No mention of wedding bells yet, but I hope that will follow.''

"And you're going to miss them," Natalie finished for her. "So you're making grouchy comments about Quent on his birthday."

"His *thirtieth* birthday," Amy added, "which is traumatic enough, as I recall from my own experience."

"Piffle." Mrs. McLanahan joined them. Her date, Hugo, the distinguished-looking but shy jeweler, hung back to watch a boat passing out to sea. "Turning thirty isn't traumatic. Turning seventy, that's another story."

"I'll bet the ninety-year-olds aren't impressed," joked Heather.

"Nor should they be." Noreen patted Amy's hand. "You know, the years don't matter if you're following your dreams. I assure you, your husband will never wish he had his twenties back. He's much better off now."

"I don't doubt that." Amy beamed at the woman. "It looks like you've got a romance of your own."

"Hugo's a sweetheart," said her friend. "We'll see where it leads. One thing I've learned is to live in the moment and let the future take care of itself."

"Good advice." Natalie put the heel of her hand to her extended abdomen. "Wow! That was quite a kick."

"Let me know if you change your mind about learning the sex," Heather said.

"We prefer to find out the old-fashioned way," Natalie told her. "Here comes the main course!"

The men arrived bearing platters. Quent, who seemed to possess infinite patience with the children, sank onto a blanket with Tara in his lap and started shredding a piece of chicken for her. Amy helped Greg pile his plate. She was beginning to know his preferences by heart.

The small group of friends settled around them on folding chairs. Noreen and her new boyfriend. Natalie and Patrick. Heather, Rob, Kitty and Aunt Mary.

It had been Amy's idea to hold a birthday party for Quent on the sand and, although the weather was iffy this time of year, everyone had liked the idea. Fortunately, they'd had a mild day, although she'd put jackets on the children as evening came.

Despite the crisp air, she felt surrounded by warmth. No need to ask why. All she had to do was glance at Quent.

Since Christmas Day, they'd drawn closer, sharing their thoughts, laughing together, resolving their differences with a loving spirit. It was going to be wonderful, she thought, to spend the rest of her life with a friend who was also her true love.

A boom! from offshore nearly sent her flying out of her seat. "What was that?"

"Look, Mommy!" Greg pointed at the darkness above the ocean. "Sky flowers."

A fountain of white sparks pierced the deep blue expanse. An instant later, a series of bangs heralded an explosion of reds and blues.

"Fireworks!" she said. "Look, Greg, aren't we lucky?"

"Luck had nothing to do with it." Hoisting Tara onto his hip, Quent moved closer.

"You arranged this?" she asked in disbelief, as colors splashed the sky. "What an enormous undertaking!"

"I've always wanted fireworks on my birthday," he said. "Besides, this is the one-month anniversary of our wedding. These are for you, too."

"Thank you! I love it."

Their friends chorused their appreciation. "My baby's really jumping now." Natalie patted her bulge. "He or she can hear the whole thing."

Greg climbed onto Amy's lap, and Quent took the chair beside her, holding their daughter. The children stared upward, too enchanted to speak. As a palette of light blossomed above them, Amy felt as if she were floating among stars.

Close to her ear, Quent said, "It's only a token, Amy. This is nothing compared to the enchantment you bring to my life."

He slipped one arm around her. Safely enfolded in her husband's love, Amy rested her head on his shoulder and watched the fireworks paint the sky with magic.

* * * * *

*Don't miss the final installment
in Jacqueline Diamond's*
THE BABIES OF DOCTORS CIRCLE *series!*

*Look for PROGNOSIS: A BABY? MAYBE
coming in July 2003 from
Harlequin American Romance.*

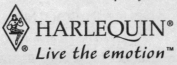

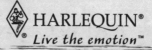

New York Times bestselling author

STELLA CAMERON

JANICE KAY JOHNSON

WRONG TURN

Every day, things happen to change the course of our lives...and at the time, we might not even notice.

A compelling romance about the decisions that count— even the wrong ones.

WRONG TURN is available in May 2003, wherever books are sold.

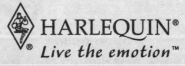

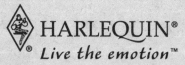